To Spencer, John, Steven, Jared, and Isaac,

who once asked me for a bedtime story

about superheroes, and refused to take

no for an answer.

1.

WHO GAVE GREAT-AUNT SILVA MATILDA FIZZY LEMONADE?

I woke up on the worst day of my entire life fully expecting it to be the best day of my entire life. Sometimes life is funny that way. And when I say *funny*, I don't mean funny as in, "Ha-ha, that's a good joke, thanks for sharing." I mean funny as in someone coming to your birthday party, punching you in the stomach, and then stealing your new puppy.

Which I guess is to say it's really not that funny at all.

I remember everything about that day—the sights, the sounds, and the smells. More than anything, I remember the sharp stench of burning drapes.

I smelled the smoke before I actually saw the fire. It

was Monday afternoon and I was sitting on the piano bench next to my younger brother, Benny. We were in the living room, surrounded by the rest of my relatives living in Split Rock. Everyone had gathered for the big event.

The reason I had cause for alarm was not just the smoke, but because Great-aunt Silva Matilda—who sat sleeping peacefully in her wheelchair—had just burped.

And that meant trouble.

Big trouble.

"Does anybody else smell smoke?" I asked no one in particular, trying to keep my voice calm. I didn't want to alarm anyone, but I guess when you ask a question like that—*does anybody else smell smoke?*—it's bound to cause at least a little excitement.

"I smell something too," Benny said.

Uncle Chambers, sitting on the couch, stuck his nose into the air. "I don't smell any—" His eyes grew wide, and he pointed at the window. "FIRE!"

And as if that wasn't bad enough, he hollered, "We're under attack!"

It might seem strange that my uncle thought we were under attack, but actually it's not. My family gets attacked all the time. It kind of comes with the territory. But this time, as it happens, it wasn't an attack. Aunt Verna was the first to find the source of the smoke. "Oh my goodness, it's the drrrrapes!" she said, pointing toward the window.

Now that I knew where to look, I could see the flames licking at the curtains like hungry snakes, growing larger by the second.

Everybody got frantic at that point. We might have gone into full lockdown mode—because Uncle Chambers kept screaming that we were under attack—if Grandpa hadn't taken charge. He blew a puff of air into his bristling mustache and rearranged the straw hat atop his head. He started barking orders from the corner, radiating so much authority he didn't even need to stand up.

"Chambers," he said, hooking his thumbs into the straps of his overalls. "We're not under attack. Stop blabbering—you'll frighten the children. Everybody else, pipe down. I've never heard so much yammering in all my life. Jack! What are you doing standing there like a slack-jawed gopher? Set your refreshments down and try to be helpful."

My cousin Jack stood near the door, holding a plate of green-olive pie in his hands. He looked like he'd been slapped out of a daydream. He set his refreshments down, freeing up his hands.

This was important.

A lot of people can do amazing things with their hands. Some people can paint a picture that looks as pretty as you please. Others can pick up a hammer and nails and build an entire house. But I'm willing to bet you've never seen anything like what Cousin Jack can do. You see, Jack's last name is Bailey. And Baileys are different. Not just a little bit different. A *lot* different.

Jack held out his right hand—though actually either one would have worked—and a stream of water poured from his palm. It was like those fancy fountains where the dolphin statue shoots water out of its mouth. Cousin Jack's aim was true. Water struck fire, which sputtered and died in a hiss of steam. The drapes—now black and smoking—were drenched.

Baileys are super.

"Who gave Great-aunt Silva Matilda fizzy lemonade?" Grandpa asked. He said it in the same way that you would say, "Who smeared chocolate pudding all over the dog?" His face was stern. "Didn't I tell everybody the bubbles make her burp?"

You see, Great-aunt Silva Matilda is a Bailey, too. I've been told that in the "good old days" she could breathe fire just like a dragon in a fairy tale. She could knock over a supervillain at fifty paces and brown a marshmallow at a hundred. And though her crime-fighting days are long behind her—as are her s'mores-making days—she still has a little bit of power left.

"Point her toward the fireplace, will you, Rafter?" Grandpa asked me. "She'll likely be burping up a storm all afternoon."

I got up and wheeled Great-aunt Silva Matilda over to the fireplace, making sure to point her toward the bricks. In spite of all the ruckus, I watched the clock like a hawk. At that point, I still very much believed that today would be the best day of my life.

Great-aunt Silva Matilda first burped at 4:02. By the time the fire was out, it was 4:03. And by the time I'd situated Great-aunt Silva Matilda by the fireplace and returned to my seat at the piano, the clock on the wall read 4:04.

Nineteen minutes. In nineteen minutes, I would finally have a superpower of my own.

That is why I expected it to be the best day of my life.

At 4:23 in the afternoon, on February 29, any Bailey age twelve or older gets a superpower. Benny was twelve, and I was thirteen, so we'd both get a power at the same time. No one in our family knows why it happens to us—why the universe chose the Bailey family to be the defenders of everything right and good. We don't question why. We just accept the responsibility.

Benny started counting on his fingers. After a few seconds of flicking them up and down, he turned to me and asked, "How much longer?"

I looked at the clock, hoping it had advanced another minute. It hadn't. "Nineteen minutes."

"Why do we get our powers at four twenty-three?"

he asked. "I wish it were at four thirty. That would make it easier to do the math." Benny brightened. "Actually, it would be better if we got our powers at four o'clock, because then we'd already be superheroes!"

Benny flexed his muscles, and I hid a smile.

Benny threw the clock a sour look. "I think that thing's busted. I'm going to get something to eat." He left the room.

I counted the number of superheroes in the living room. There were eleven total, counting Great-aunt Silva Matilda. In just a few minutes, we'd have thirteen. I couldn't help it. I was grinning like an idiot.

Benny returned with a plate of traditional leap-year refreshments—green-olive pie, toasted buckwheat, and a glass of fizzy pink lemonade.

4:08. I couldn't sit still for another fifteen minutes. I walked over to the window and looked at the gray sky and gray snow. I guess maybe I should've seen that as an omen—all that gray.

My sixteen-year-old cousin Jessie played with two of my younger cousins outside. In our family, you aren't told the family secret until you're ten—old enough to keep it safe. Jessie would keep the two younger children outside while Benny and I got our powers.

I walked back and forth in front of the window, kicking absentmindedly at pieces of charred curtain.

"Rrrrrrafter Bailey, stop that pacing," Aunt Verna

commanded. "My goodness, it isn't prrrroper!"

Aunt Verna—she has a streak of crazy running through her at least a mile wide. She sat on the sofa with her legs crossed and a napkin draped with careful precision on her lap. Her back was ramrod straight and her graying hair was pulled back into a small, tight bun. Aunt Verna is obsessed with being proper.

I thought about pacing more just to annoy her. One of the benefits of having an aunt who acts proper is that if I make her mad she can't exactly throw me over her knee and whack me a good one. That wouldn't be proper. But I didn't want any problems, especially today. So I went back to the piano and sat next to Benny. Grandpa spoke up from his chair. "Verna, how are your speech lessons coming along?"

"Oh my goodness, they arrrrrre simply divine," Aunt Verna replied. "You know, the Brrrrritish masterrred the concepts of good conduct and grrrrace hundrrrreds of yearrrrrs ago. In only two months I went frrrrom sounding like a rregular commonerrr to sounding like a Brrritish queen!"

I mumbled so only Benny could hear. "I think she went from sounding like a crazy aunt with an American accent to a crazy aunt with a bad English accent."

That made Benny snort and then choke on his olive pie. I whacked him on the back, and he recovered. Aunt Verna glared at both of us.

"What do you think yourrrrr superpowers will be, dearrrr nephews?" she asked. Her rolling *r*'s sounded more like a fake machine gun than a British aristocrat.

Benny spoke up first, his voice filled with excitement. "I want to be a Speedy. If I can run fast, maybe I'll lose my baby fat!"

Benny has always been a little bigger than me. I learned pretty fast not to wrestle with him because I usually lost. Even though he's younger, he's about the same height. He has a round face, plump cheeks, and a little extra padding around his midsection. Whenever Grandma Stevens comes over—Grandma Stevens is my mom's mom, so she doesn't know about the Bailey family secret—she always pinches Benny's cheeks and asks him when he's going to lose his baby fat. It drives Benny nuts.

Uncle Chambers, sitting next to Aunt Verna, rubbed his bald head and peered at Benny over his glasses. Uncle Chambers is missing about four teeth, and when he smiles, the black spots next to his white teeth remind me of a piano. "A Speedy? Cousin Roy is a Speedy, ain't he, Verna? Over in Oak City?" Aunt Verna likes to speak properly. Uncle Chambers . . . not so much.

"*Isn't* he, dearrrrr," Aunt Verna said. "The prrrrroper term is—"

"And ain't Cousin Roy only seventeen years old? I reckon we won't get another Speedy in the family for at least a decade—probably two." He pointed a crooked finger at Benny. "You know what we really need is another Stretcher. Great-uncle Ike is getting on in years, and he's starting to lose his elasticity. One of these days I wager he's going to snap in two. That won't be fun, I guarantee. I don't want to be around to clean up after that mess." He made a snorting sound and drained his cup of fizzy lemonade.

"I don't want to be a Stretcher," Benny said. "They don't get to wear supersuits, and they're stuck in special-ops missions because they're not that good at fighting. I'm going straight to the battles!"

"Well," Uncle Chambers said, "I think you'll be a Stretcher." He gave Benny a stern look.

Benny folded his arms, returning Uncle Chambers's look with a glare of his own.

"What about you, Rrrrrafterrrrr?" Aunt Verna asked me.

I could have told them the truth—I knew exactly what power I wanted.

Grandpa had superstrength. He could lift a car as easy as lifting a cat. But his strength was in more than just his muscles—he was an anchor. We'd just had that scare with the fire, and he'd taken care of the situation without having to put down his cup of fizzy lemonade. If a mob of supervillains had come crashing through the front door, Grandpa would have kept us all safe. He would have saved the day.

That was the power I wanted. And *that* is what I wanted to do: Save the day. I had a secret dream that someday my family would be in trouble. Nobody would be able to save them, and then I'd come along. I'd come along and save the day.

But I wasn't about to tell all that to Uncle Chambers and have him make fun of me.

"I'll be happy with whatever power I get," I said. Apparently that was a proper answer because Aunt Verna smiled and nodded.

I checked the clock again. 4:14.

Nine minutes left.

I had to find something to help kill the time. I reached into my pocket and pulled out my phone. Dad had given Benny and me phones an hour earlier. Like a lot of things we own, the phone wasn't exactly normal.

I opened up the Bailey Family Locator app, which showed a map of the city. I zoomed in until you could see our neighborhood. Flashing yellow dots showed that all twelve of the Bailey superheroes were gathered at our house, but this app would show me where everyone went, no matter where they were in the city. They'd just put a new cell tower in the city dump, and my reception had improved by leaps and bounds.

Mom came in from the kitchen. "Ah, we need more

lemonade." Her hands glowed blue, and the almost-empty bowl sitting on the coffee table floated into the kitchen. Mom left, and a moment later the bowl floated back to the coffee table, filled with pink liquid.

Dad appeared in the doorway. "Let's get going!" he shouted, rubbing his hands together. He turned and faced the kitchen. "Everybody into the living room. Hup, hup, look lively."

Benny squirmed next to me on the piano bench. "It's almost time," he said, his voice quivering with enthusiasm. "Rafter, it's almost time. I can't believe it's almost time!"

I could feel my heart thumping against the inside of my chest. It felt like a trapped animal trying to break out of a cage. The rest of the family began to squeeze their way in around the furniture.

Rodney, my older brother, came into the room and took a seat. He rested a tablet computer on his knees and poked at it while he waited. Sometimes Mom gets after Rodney for spending too much time on his computers, but since his superpower is all in his brain, he has a good excuse. Rodney manages our family's entire computer network and security system.

Anxious murmurs filled the air. It reminded me of the few minutes right before a baseball game starts. Everybody in the stands is watching and waiting and you know that any second the batter is going to approach the plate, the pitcher will throw the ball, and the game will be underway.

I checked the clock.

4:21.

My stomach lurched.

Dad was stuck at the door of the living room. He tried stepping around relatives before he finally gave up and used his power. He floated to the ceiling, hovered to the middle of the room, then landed gently on the floor.

If I didn't mention it, Dad can fly.

Dad never passes up the opportunity to make a speech (or a lecture, depending on the situation). He cleared his throat, and the room fell silent. "Thank you all for coming," he said. "It's nice to be surrounded by family on a day like this. It's our hope that with the addition of these new superheroes, we'll finally be able to triumph over our archenemies—those vile, evil, dirty, rotten supervillains—the Johnsons!"

Dad shook his fist, and a wave of grumbling spread across the room. Several of my relatives shook their fists in reply.

I know the name *Johnson* doesn't exactly sound like the best name for supervillains, but it's all part of their plan. With a normal name, they fit right in with the regular citizens of the city. It's quite sneaky when you think about it.

4:22.

"Ever since this noble feud began back in . . . oh, who can remember when it began, really . . . anyway, ever since then we have kept the citizens of Split Rock safe from those villains. And we'll continue until we best them!"

Everyone nodded, a few of my relatives clapped, and Aunt Verna said, "Hearrrrr, hearrrrr, my good chap."

Dad didn't get any further with his speech. The clock—which had been synched up with an atomic one on the internet—flipped to 4:23. The hoping, the waiting, and the wondering were about to come to an end.

Starting with Benny.

"I'm feeling something weird," he said. "It's like a tingling in my face!" Benny rubbed his face and squirmed on the bench.

"Hot dog, it's happening!" Dad shouted. "Rafter, do you feel anything?"

I shook my head, then had a horrible thought. "Hey . . . am I adopted?"

Dad shook his head. "And even if you were, as soon as you're legally a Bailey, you get a power on the next leap year."

This was true. That's how Mom got her power—after she married Dad.

Benny's eyes were shut tight. He didn't look like he was in pain, but he didn't look comfortable, either.

He tilted his head to one side and closed his eyes even tighter. His eyebrows scrunched together, and he hugged his arms across his chest.

I thought I saw a flash of light. Like a light bulb had gone off. Or maybe lightning. I looked out the window but there was only gray sky.

Benny opened his eyes.

"It's over," he said. His voice was a whisper. He had a faraway look. "I have it. I know what my power is."

Benny looked like he'd just seen an ice cream truck drive off a cliff. My first thought was that he hadn't gotten the speed he wanted. But deep down, I think I knew even then that it was far worse than that.

"Benny," Mom said, her voice filled with excitement. "What is your power? What did you get?"

"I . . . uh . . ." Benny said, and I heard a soft pop.

At the time, I didn't even wonder what the pop was.

My own power had started.

Getting a superpower is difficult to describe.

Benny was right; it started with a tingling feeling in the head. Then the feeling worked its way through my entire body as energy surged through my arms, legs, and chest.

I thought I saw another burst of light outside. I didn't have time to think about it because the tingling sensation became stronger and stronger until it felt like an electrical current surging right through my bones. My flesh buzzed with power. Pressure built up inside my head, and then . . . something clicked.

This next part is the hardest to explain. The only way I can describe it is like somebody stuck a flash drive into my head and it transferred information directly to my brain. My mind filled with knowledge and insight. Another wave of energy washed over me, and then . . . it was over.

I sat on the piano bench, stunned. I knew what my superpower was. I knew how it worked. I knew every last part of it, inside and out.

And I knew I would have it for the rest of my life.

This was supposed to be a special day. It was supposed to be the best day of my life. The day I was going to become super.

Only . . . I didn't.

Devastated, I jumped off the piano bench and ran from the room.

2

I'M ALWAYS AFRAID OF GETTING LAVA DOWN MY TIGHTS

I didn't cry.

I wanted to, and I left the living room because I was worried I would start, but I never did. I got to my room, closed the door, and pulled at my hair. Ten seconds later, Mom was there, knocking on my door.

"Rafter, come on out, honey."

I stared at the door and fought down the tears. Thirteen-year-olds don't cry. And superheroes definitely don't.

But then again, I wasn't exactly a superhero.

"Come on, sweetie," Mom said. "Everybody's waiting."

"I'd rather not come out, Mom," I said, keeping my voice steady. "I think I'd like a little alone time."

"Rafter, don't make me count to ten," she said, her voice firm.

I closed my eyes and hoped Mom was joking. I wasn't six. "One."

And with that, I knew she'd won. I refused to be treated like a child. I steeled myself, marched to the door, and opened it. I walked past Mom and made my way to the living room. My relatives sat there, as quiet as spectators at a golf game. Five minutes earlier an excited buzz had filled the room. Now there was just awkward silence.

Benny looked as miserable as I felt. He sat on the bench, his head resting in his hands. This morning the world was ours for the taking. We were going to be heroes.

I focused on walking to the piano. I didn't look at anyone.

"Okay, boys," Dad said, and I heard the same firmness in his voice that I'd just heard from Mom. "I know you may not have gotten the exact power you wanted, but that's no excuse for moping around. When I was your age, I wanted to be a human torch. I loved to start things on fire and watch them burn. All that heat, and crackling, and . . . and power! One time when I was eight, I took some matches, some WD-40, and a stack of old tractor tires—"

"Uh, dear," Mom said. "I don't think we need to go into that right now."

Dad stopped. "Oh, right. Of course. Let me go on the record saying it's never safe to play with matches. And Smokey the Bear really knows his stuff."

He cleared his throat. "Anyway, I didn't get the power I wanted, but flying has worked out just fine. Whatever powers you boys have, you'll learn to use them in the fight against the Johnsons." He shook his fist.

Relatives murmured their agreement and mumbled under their breath about the rottenness of the Johnsons. I kept my eyes on the floor.

"Benny," Dad said. "You got your power first. What is it? What is your ability?"

My brother dropped his gaze to his lap. His voice sounded sad. "I don't think you want to know."

"Yes," Dad said firmly, "I do."

"Well, I don't think I want to tell you."

"Nonsense!" Dad boomed, as if he were making a speech for citizens and not his son. "The universe has chosen you and me—all of us—to become superheroes." Dad pointed a finger high into the air. "We don't know why the universe chose us. We don't even know where these powers come from. And we certainly can't pretend to understand why they come on February twenty-ninth at four twenty-three in the afternoon."

Several relatives nodded vigorously. "But we use these powers for good," Dad said. "Always for good! We fight evil wherever it may rear its ugly head. We are Baileys! We are superheroes!" Dad paused for dramatic effect, and then, in the most commanding superhero voice he could muster, he said, "Benjamin Sinclair Bailey, what superpower do you have that will aid us in this fight?"

Benny looked up at Dad. Complete silence settled over the room. Benny's voice was a whisper, but it carried to every person in the room.

"I can turn my belly button from an innie to an outie."

Nobody said anything for a full ten seconds. Then everybody started yelling at once.

"That's not a superpower!"

"Surely you're mistaken."

"Is it high powered? Can you shoot out belly-button lint?"

"Currrious, verrrry currrrious!"

"*Quiet!*" Dad's voice broke through the shouting, and my family settled down. Everyone looked around in disbelief, but all eyes eventually fell on Benny. He returned their gaze with a face carved of stone. Then without breaking eye contact, he lifted his shirt. He had a normal-looking belly button—an innie.

With a soft pop, his belly button popped out of his stomach. It was still ordinary looking, but now it was an outie. "Uh . . ." was all Dad could manage.

Mom asked, "Can you change it back?"

With a pop, Benny's belly button retreated back inside

his stomach like a frightened turtle.

Benny pulled his shirt down. "Ta-da," he said weakly.

I looked at my brother, and for a moment our eyes met. He looked disappointed. No. Not just disappointed. Full of complete and utter despair. Like he'd been broken.

I knew exactly how he felt. Everyone was staring at us, but I didn't care. I put my arm around my little brother and gave his shoulder a squeeze.

"We'll figure this out," I said, low enough that only Benny could hear. I didn't know if we *would* figure this out—I didn't even know if there was anything *to* figure out—but I had to say something.

"Um, Rafter, honey?" Mom said, and I heard a nervous lilt in her voice. "What about you? What's your power?"

I didn't know exactly how to describe it. I decided a demonstration would be better. I took a deep breath.

"Dad, can you get me a couple of matches?" I asked.

"Oh!" Dad said. "You got a fire power. Lucky you!"

Yeah. Lucky me.

Dad left to get matches. I scooted down the piano bench so I could be within arm's length of the couch.

Dad returned. "Here you go." He dropped a dozen matches into my hand.

I took a deep breath.

"These matches are the kind that you can only strike on the box, right?"

Dad nodded. "Safety first, that's a family motto."

There wasn't any way to make it sound incredible, so I just said it. "I can also strike them on polyester."

I took a match, leaned over, and slid it along the couch. The match flared to life. I let it burn for a few seconds and then blew it out.

Every superhero in the room stared at me. "Only polyester?" Mom asked, her voice small in the silence of the room.

I slid a new match along the leather seat of the piano bench. Nothing. I slid it along my shirt. Nothing.

"Yep."

Dad walked over and plucked a match from my hand. He struck it several times along the couch. No fire. He passed it to me. I flicked it against the couch, and the match burst into flames.

Uncle Chambers cleared his throat. "Uh, William," he said to Dad. "I've got several leisure suits back at the house . . . made from high-quality polyester. If you need them . . ."

Aunt Verna stood, and then—as if on cue—everyone started to get up. A few people muttered congratulations, but I knew nobody really meant it.

I heard Dad mumbling to himself. "I wonder if the other cousins . . ." He got up, pulled his phone out of his pocket, and left the room.

Rodney started to follow him, then stopped. "Don't

worry, guys," he said. "Maybe I can design some special weapons on my computer. You know, to make up for your . . ." He looked uncomfortable, then left without finishing.

Somehow, Rodney treating me like a weakling—like a regular citizen—made me feel like I'd been punched in the stomach. In a family where your power is everything, Benny and I had just moved to the bottom of the pile. We were nobodies.

I put my elbows on my knees, and my head in my hands.

Mom pulled Great-aunt Silva Matilda away from the fireplace. The movement caused her to burp, sending out a small flash of yellow flame.

"Even Great-aunt Silva Matilda's belching is more powerful than we are," Benny mumbled.

I stared at the floor and listened as my relatives put on their coats, gathered children from outside, and headed to their cars. Soon, the only noise was the ticking of the clock. I barely noticed.

When Grandpa spoke, I almost fell off the bench. I thought he'd left with the others, but he still sat in the easy chair, his feet resting on an ottoman. "Look at you two boys," he said, "sitting on that bench. Sniffling and pining away like a couple of namby-pambies."

I didn't know what *pining* meant, but I could guess.

It might sound like I've got the meanest grandpa in the world, but that's just his style. He'll step in and help you when you really need it, but if you've got a hangnail or a small splinter, he's probably not the best guy to go to for sympathy. He'll likely just whack you on the back of the head and tell you stop your bellyaching.

"You saw what happened, Grandpa," Benny said. "We got worthless powers. The only thing I can do is pop out my navel half an inch."

Grandpa snorted and then puckered his lips—his white mustache reaching up toward his nose. "I'm going to let you boys in on a little secret," he said. "I've been alive for almost sixty-five years now. I've thought a lot about these powers our family gets. What I've noticed is that these powers don't make us super. Technically, if you want to get right down to it, we're all just a bunch of freaks. I mean, what normal person breathes fire out of their mouth? That's something you'd expect to see in a circus or a heartburn commercial, not in real life."

Grandpa put his feet on the floor. "Listen," he said. "Do you know what the Latin root for *super* is?"

I shook my head.

"The root of *super* is *soup*," Grandpa said, "which means 'tasty liquid.'" He paused. "Wait, that doesn't sound right . . . actually, forget Latin. Let's stick to English. The definition of *super* is 'above' or 'beyond.' Now,

I don't know anybody who can pop their belly button in and out, Benny. Nor do I know anybody who can strike a match without having to leave the comfort of the couch. Those abilities are above and beyond what is natural, and therefore you boys have superpowers."

"Yeah, but Grandpa—" I started.

"No buts," Grandpa said. "End of story. However, like I was saying a moment ago, having a superpower doesn't make you a superhero. *That* you have to earn."

I didn't understand at all.

"Did you know," Grandpa said, "that sometimes— not always, but sometimes—we Baileys get a power that makes up for a weakness?" Grandpa kicked the ottoman to the side and leaned forward in his chair. He shook a wrinkled finger at me and Benny.

"Take your cousin Jack, for instance. His power has saved this family many times. The Johnsons," Grandpa shook his fist, "have this pesky lady that can shoot lava. She's a real problem. You're minding your own business— maybe you have a Johnson in a headlock and you're beating on him, right? The next thing you know, you've got hot lava flying around your head. I'll be honest, I'm always afraid of getting lava down my tights."

Benny stifled a snort next to me. Grandpa didn't notice.

"Jack sprays the lava with his water. Turns it into harmless pebbles. Darnedest thing I've ever seen."

Grandpa rubbed his chin. "But I was making a point, and now I've gone and forgotten it. Let's see . . . oh yes. Did you know that Jack is terrified of fire?"

That didn't sound right. Superheroes weren't afraid of anything.

"Didn't you see him when the drapes were all smoking and a-cracklin'?" Grandpa asked. "He stood there like a skunk caught in an outhouse. I had to yell and wake him up. If he's not focused, his fear gets the best of him. He's been afraid of fire since the day he was born. You should see the video from Jack's first birthday party. His mother lights the candle on the cake and puts it in front of him. Little Jack throws a fit and he pushes the whole cake off the table—screams like a baby the entire time. Actually, I guess he was a baby, so that makes sense. Anyway, it's the darnedest thing I've ever seen."

"I thought Jack squirting lava with his water was the darnedest thing you've ever seen," I said.

Grandpa ignored me.

Benny folded his arms across his chest. "So I can push my belly button in and out, and that's going to help make up for some weakness I have?"

Grandpa looked hard at Benny. "Haven't you heard a word I've been saying?" he asked. "It's not the powers that make us superheroes—it's what we *do* with those powers." He stood up. "You want to be a superhero? You have to earn it. I'm only going to say this once, because you boys are smart enough to get it on the first go-round.

"When evil has you whipped, and you don't have an ounce of strength left in your tired old bones, when everybody around you has given up or is cowering in fear, when you're down on your knees and the only sure thing is death, when all is lost and hope is nowhere to be found . . ." Grandpa leaned over, his face level with Benny's and mine. "At that horrible moment, a superhero stands, turns so he can look evil right in the eyes, and says, 'Is that the best you can do?'"

Grandpa straightened up. "Iron resolve. Ferocious courage. And a healthy dose of insanity. *That's* what makes a superhero. Not some amazing power."

Grandpa turned and left the room.

✳

I went to bed early, and Benny did too. The clock on our nightstand read 8:19. Frost on the window turned the landscape outside sparkly and sharp. The moon hung high in the sky, giving a pale white glow to the snow-covered yard.

My brain raced. Ever since my tenth birthday, I'd been preparing for this day. Preparing to become super, fight the Johnsons, and most of all, save the day.

You couldn't save the day with matches and polyester.

I heard Benny get out of bed. He was looking through one of his drawers.

"What are you doing?" I sat up in bed.

Benny pulled out a marble.

"I just thought of something," he said. "What if my belly button is high powered? It does pop out pretty quick. What if I plugged it up with this marble, and then shot it out? If it came out like a bullet, that could be something useful."

He lifted his shirt and stuck the marble into his belly button. It promptly fell back out.

"Dang it!" Benny exclaimed. "It's not exactly staying in."

Benny tried several times to get the marble to stay in his navel.

"Try lying on your back," I said. "And then put the marble on top of your belly button. That way gravity will hold it in place."

"But how can I shoot anybody if I'm lying on my back?" Benny asked. "I could only point it straight up."

I shrugged. "Just try it."

Benny got down on the floor and lay on his back. "I guess I could always pretend to be knocked out. And then when a Johnson leans over to gloat, I could shoot him."

Lifting his shirt, Benny placed the marble carefully on his belly button. It glistened in the darkness.

"Okay," Benny said. "Here goes nothing."

I heard a soft pop. The marble flipped up about two inches, and then fell harmlessly to the floor and rolled under the bed.

"Dang it!" Benny sat up and his shoulders slumped.

"It was a good try," I said. "It was some good super-hero thinking."

"I wanted it to work," Benny said. "Because otherwise we're in huge trouble."

"What do you mean?" I asked.

Benny climbed back in bed. His next words dropped like a bucket of ice down the back of my pajamas. "Juanita Johnson."

Benny and I attend Split Rock Middle School. Dad says that we'll learn the important stuff during our super-hero studies, but we go to school so we can blend in with the citizens of the community. The problem is, so does Juanita Johnson—supervillain.

I'd never liked the idea of having to go to school with a supervillain. She was in the eighth grade with me, but I'd always figured that no matter what power she got, Benny and I could stand together.

But now . . .

"She got her power today too," I said.

"Yeah." Benny said. "But we can still handle her, right?"

I didn't answer. Juanita and I had a class together—algebra. School was about to get dangerous.

I'd started drifting off when I heard my parents talking in the next room. The walls in our house are pretty solid, so I could only hear a few words here and there. But a few words were enough.

"... six nephews and nieces ... Oak City, Farmington, Trenton ... none of them got a real power ... nobody knows ..."

I didn't hear anything for a few minutes, but then Dad spoke two words that cut through the darkness.

"... completely worthless ..."

It took a long time to fall asleep.

3

DRINK YOUR GOAT'S MILK

Lying in bed, half asleep, I figured I'd had a nightmare. A nightmare where Benny and I had gotten worthless powers. I struggled to remember what our real powers were.

Benny's alarm rang. He slid off the bed and fell in a heap onto the floor. His head poked out from under the covers. "Is it morning?" I heard a pop.

His belly button. It hadn't been a dream.

"Yeah, it's morning," I said.

Mom's voice echoed through the house. "Boys? Breakfast!"

Fighting a wave of despair, I got up, went to our walk-in closet, and stepped inside. I quickly got dressed and then grabbed my shoes and socks. When I came out of the closet, I saw Benny on the floor, his belly and face pressed flat against the carpet. He pushed against the carpet with his hands.

"What are you doing?" I asked.

"Push-ups!" he said, gasping as his plump body rose into the air. His arms shuddered under the weight, and his whole frame shook with effort.

I had a thought. "Have you tried doing push-ups with your belly button?" I asked. "Maybe your navel is like some kind of amazing unstoppable force, and you could—"

"Already tried it," Benny grunted. "Didn't work."

I sighed and began pulling on my socks and shoes. "So why are you doing push-ups?"

Benny collapsed to the floor and rolled onto his back. "I want to be as strong as possible when we get our supersuits. The more muscles I have, the better I'll be able to fight." Benny's breathing came in puffs—his face was flushed.

"How many push-ups did you do?" I asked.

Benny sat up. "Five, but I bet I can get to six by tomorrow." He stood and flexed his muscles. "Oh yeah, I can tell I'm getting stronger already."

I didn't have the heart to tell Benny that the ability to do a lot of push-ups would never come in handy when fighting supervillains.

I went downstairs, finding the same breakfast we had every day of our lives. I can tell you a hundred advantages of living in a superhero family—the cool devices, the secret identities, the off chance of meeting with high-up government officials. But the superhero diet is not one of them.

"Ah!" said Dad, striding into the room. "The breakfast of superheroes!" He dished up some rice in a bowl, sprinkled spearmint leaves on top, and poured a pint of warm goat's milk over the green-and-white lump. He shoveled it into his mouth and smiled.

I dropped into my seat and stared at the white blob. I could barely stomach this food on a good day, and today was not a good day.

"Can Benny and I have cold cereal?" I finally asked. "Since we're not going to be superheroes?"

"Nonsense!" Mom said. "You're superheroes, just like the rest of us."

"This food keeps us in tip-top shape," Dad said, his mouth full of rice. "Both mental and physical. It's a perfect balance of nutrients and vitamins. And the spearmint keeps your breath minty fresh."

"I'd rather have cereal," I said. "The kind with marsh-mallows. Or what about eggs and bacon? I still remember the last time I had bacon—it was like heaven in my belly."

We eat regular food when we have to blend in. I'd eaten

bacon four times in my life, and every time was memorable.

"Drink your goat's milk," Dad said.

I didn't eat anything. I had a big chunk of gloom in my gut, and it didn't want company.

Benny came downstairs and dished up a large helping of rice and goat's milk. "I need extra energy because I'm doing push-ups," he explained.

Rodney had already left for school. Everyone ate in silence until Dad finally cleared his throat. "I thought you boys might want to know that I called around to some of the neighboring cities. Spoke to some of my cousins, an uncle. . . . Yesterday everybody who was old enough got . . . interesting powers."

I remembered what he'd said last night and wondered if he really meant *worthless* powers.

"Like what?" Benny asked.

"Let me think," Dad said. "Spencer is the son of one of my cousins. He has the ability to knit. He can't do it fast, and he can't knit anything useful like steel cables or carbon nano-strings. In fact, he can only knit sweaters."

"Sweaters?" I asked.

Dad nodded. "And they don't even fit people. Just small dogs. Toy poodles. Chihuahuas. Or puppies, I guess."

"His power is the ability to knit small dog sweaters?"

"Yep," Dad said. "And your second cousin Anya . . . She sees a timer above everybody's head. It tells her how long it's been since the person last shampooed their hair."

I couldn't believe it. "Why is this happening?"

Nobody answered my question.

I looked at the clock. In ten minutes, the bus would stop in front of our house. Benny and I would climb aboard. Eight minutes after that we'd stop and pick up Juanita Johnson. Because of our worthless powers, she would have the perfect opportunity to . . .

I couldn't believe I'd been so slow.

"Of course!" I said.

"What is it, son?" Mom asked. Benny and Dad both stopped eating to stare at me.

I saw a glimmer of hope. A flicker of light in a black cave.

"We didn't get our real powers yesterday," I said, having a hard time talking through my excitement. "Somehow the Johnsons messed things up. They gave us these worthless ones instead. It's so obvious."

All I got for my grand revelation was a, "Can someone please pass the spearmint?"

Dad looked skeptical. "I don't think that's how it works," he said. "It's the universe that gives us these powers. The Johnsons can't interfere with that. And you're forgetting to shake your fist when you say *Johnsons*." Dad shook his fist—twice.

I shook my fist, but only because I didn't want an argument. "This is all part of their plan," I said. "They took away our powers so Juanita can get us at school."

"Juanita can't do anything at school—you know that," Dad said. "Supervillains have to maintain a secret identity just like we do. Stay in public places, and you'll be fine. Just don't make the mistake of getting caught alone with this girl."

"We could skip school," I suggested. "At least until we know what's going on."

"Rafter, honey," Mom said. "Do you have another algebra test you're trying to get out of? I know how you struggle with math."

"I don't struggle with . . ." I took a deep breath. "Dad, will you at least call Grandpa and see what he thinks?" I remembered something. "Yesterday, right before we got our powers, I saw a flash of light. Did anybody else see that?"

Blank stares.

"I think you might be grasping at straws, son," Dad said.

"I'm not," I said. "I thought I saw a flash of light when Benny got his power. And then again when I got mine. Like lightning."

Dad raised his eyebrows. "From outside?"

"Yeah." I tried to remember exactly what I'd seen. "It seemed like it was coming from the right . . . and maybe a little behind our house."

"Like from downtown?" Dad said.

"No," I said. "More toward the mountain. Like out Highway Eighty-nine. In the direction of the dump."

Dad went back to his breakfast. "Don't you think if there was really a flash of light somebody else would have seen it?" Dad said. "There were a dozen of us in that room."

"Everybody was looking at Benny and me," I said. "We were the only ones facing the window. Just tell Grandpa about the light. That might be important."

Dad sighed. "I'll talk to Grandpa. I just don't want to see you get your hopes up and then have them dashed again."

I grabbed some food after all. I knew I was right. Grandpa would put together a team and we'd figure out what was going on. Somehow I would get my power, and I would find a way to save the day.

I finished my breakfast and then went to get my backpack.

The Johnsons had stolen my dreams. The Johnsons had taken my power.

It was time to take it back.

4

IF HE OFFERS CANDY, DON'T TAKE IT

Benny and I stood on the corner of Camel Street and Alpaca Way, waiting for the bus. The sidewalks had been shoveled and were clear of snow. I breathed out slowly and watched the mist disappear in the cold March air. Benny and I stood away from the other kids so we could talk in relative privacy.

"So how are we going to get Juanita?" my brother asked.

I looked at him in surprise. "What are you talking about? We're not going to get Juanita. You heard Dad, we have to stay away from her."

"How come?" Benny asked. "We're superheroes. Fighting supervillains is what we do."

"Uh, have you forgotten we got worthless powers?" I asked Benny in a low voice. He didn't look too happy at being reminded. "We have to wait for Grandpa and Dad to figure out what the Johnsons have done. Once we get our real powers, then we can worry about Juanita."

Benny scowled. "I still think we can handle her."

The bus came and we climbed on board.

Mike Slade, one of my best friends, waved me over to his seat. We hadn't sat together on the bus for at least a year. I didn't know why he'd chosen today to have me sit by him, but I walked over feeling pleased. I missed talking with him.

"Hey, Rafter," Mike said. "Sorry, I wasn't waving at you. I was waving at Skyler behind you."

My face turned red. "Yeah," I said. "I knew that. I just wanted to say hi."

"Oh," Mike said. "Hi."

I walked to the back of the bus and sat by Benny, my face still burning. Mike and I used to hang out all the time, but then things changed when I learned about my family secret. Mike's dad is a police officer, and the police don't really like superheroes. We fight crime for free, and in fact, with the exception of the Johnsons, there aren't a lot of criminals left in our city. Bad guys know if they do something wrong, they're going to get caught. A lot of people have even said we don't need the police anymore.

So while I was looking forward to becoming a super-hero like my dad, Mike saw *his* dad always worrying about his job. Mike never suspected I was a superhero, but it was hard to hear him saying nasty things about superheroes. About my family.

Being a superhero can be lonely. Luckily, I had Benny.

"Did you know"—I realized that my brother was talking to me—"that lumberjacks can grow facial hair at three times the normal speed of a regular man?"

"Uh . . ." I wasn't sure what to say. "I don't think that's right. Where did you hear that?"

"I read it in a book." Benny tapped my arm. "This is Juanita's stop."

Two boys and a girl climbed on the bus, but Juanita was nowhere in sight.

Benny leaned over and whispered in my ear, "Maybe she got flying, and she doesn't need to take the bus."

I didn't like it. I didn't like it one bit.

We rode the rest of the way in silence.

The bus stopped at our school and we climbed off. Benny and I got off last. Benny bent over to tie his shoe-lace and the bus pulled away. Something across the street caught my attention.

"Hey," I said, pointing. "Look at that guy over there."

A man stood across the street behind a tree. He looked silly, because the trunk wasn't more than a few inches thick. In fact, the whole tree was probably only eight feet tall. Benny and I could see him clearly. He wore a trench coat over a pair of striped pajamas, and his nose was red from the cold. He had a large stocking cap and a fake beard. I could see the elastic strap that kept the hairy mass pressed against his face.

"Stranger danger!" Benny hissed. "If he offers candy, don't take it."

I didn't expect the man to offer us candy. A single word went through my head. . . .

Johnson.

The man stepped away from the tree and walked toward us. He held something out in front of him, pointing it directly at Benny and me.

I pulled Benny behind me, and then got a better look at the object in the man's hand. I let out my breath.

"It's a phone," I said, moving backward, pushing Benny toward the school.

"Is he a Johnson?" Benny asked.

"Not one I recognize," I said. "Maybe he's from out of town."

The man punched a button on his phone. He was now close enough that I heard it beep. The man peered at the phone, then threw back his head and laughed.

It only took a second for me to understand. Somehow that phone told him what our powers were. My face grew hot.

"Come on," I said, grabbing Benny by the arm. "Let's get to school."

"What just happened?" Benny asked. "What did he do?"

"That was a Johnson." I shook my fist long and hard. "And it means I was right at breakfast. He had some sensor on his phone. One that told him what our powers were. That's why he was laughing. The villains messed up our powers, and they sent somebody down here to make sure it worked."

The man still howled with laughter behind us. I resisted the urge to turn around and chase him down. What would I do if I caught him? He wasn't wearing any polyester, and I didn't have any matches.

An electronic buzz cut through the air. First period.

"Remember what Dad said," I told Benny. "Keep to public places, hang out in the library during recess, and stay in class. Just because Juanita wasn't on the bus doesn't mean she's not here."

Benny gave me a thumbs-up. "Piece of cake," he said, and turned and left for class.

I left for history. When history was finished, I braced myself. I walked into algebra, ready for anything. My stomach felt all twisted up inside.

But Juanita wasn't in her seat when I got there, and she wasn't there when I left. In fact, I didn't see her all that day.

The twisted feeling in my stomach grew worse.

5

IN THE BAG, BENNY. IN THE BAG.

I'll admit it—Juanita's absence made me more than a little nervous. I don't like being in the dark. But Tuesday night, something happened that turned my nervous feeling into complete terror.

It went like this.

Tuesday night I got in bed and fell asleep. I awoke to a loud siren blaring through the house.

Bwooop—Bwoooop—Bwoooop

I've heard this noise a hundred times, but I never get used to it. I woke up with my heart trying to claw its way out of my throat.

The Battle Alarm.

I turned on my reading lamp, hopped out of bed, and

crossed over to Benny. He's a heavy sleeper. I made the mistake of letting him sleep through a battle once, and he still hasn't forgiven me.

"Benny, the Johnsons are attacking!" I yelled into his ear. "We've got a battle on our hands."

He opened his eyes, but still didn't look awake. "I don't wanna carry that donkey. . . ." He tried pulling the covers over his head, but I shook him again.

"Benny, a battle!"

I watched as understanding spread across his face. "A battle?"

I nodded.

"Hot dog!" Benny said. "Maybe we'll get put on the squad! Do you think they have our supersuits ready?"

Going to your first battle is a big deal. After you get your power, you usually go to the very next fight. But it had only been a little over twenty-four hours since Benny and I had gotten our powers, which meant there hadn't been time to design supersuits that would work with our powers. And now that I thought about it, how do you design a suit around a belly-button power?

Benny leaped off his bed, grabbed his bathrobe, and raced out the door. "It's like our birthday!" he shouted over his shoulder.

The alarm fell silent. I grabbed my bathrobe and slippers and followed Benny out the door.

Downstairs, Benny bounced through the house like a hyperactive puppy. He kept shouting into the darkness, asking where his supersuit was.

Dad walked into the room and turned on the lights. "Rodney is downstairs getting the orders," he said. "Everyone else, out to the backyard. We have to make this look convincing."

I don't know how the rest of my relatives handle battle alarms, but every time ours goes off, we march outside to pretend like we're performing a fire drill. We have to make it look believable in case any of the neighbors wake up. In fact, before I knew the family secret, that's what I thought too. That Dad was just really careful when it came to fires.

We walked outside. The cold air bit at my ears and cheeks, and the inside of my nose froze.

Most of our neighbors sleep through the alarm. Or if they don't, they never say anything about it. But one neighbor—Mr. Cooper—doesn't much care for the whole piercing-alarm-in-the-middle-of-the-night routine.

"Hopefully he'll sleep through it this time," Dad said, looking at Mr. Cooper's house. My father didn't have any shoes on, but his feet hovered a few inches above the snowy ground. One of the many benefits of being able to fly.

A light flared in Mr. Cooper's window.

"Light sleeper," Dad grumbled.

I watched as a balding head appeared at the glass.

After a bit of struggling, Mr. Cooper pulled open the window and stuck his head outside.

"Evening, Carl." Dad waved, his voice cheerful and steady. "Or is it morning? I didn't look at the clock."

"William!" Mr. Cooper shouted. "What in the—"

"Uh-uh, no obscenities," Dad said. "We have little Benny out here with us."

"Hey," Benny said. "I'm not little—I've been doing push-ups."

"I meant *little* as in *young*," Dad said.

"I've heard cursing before," Benny said. "I'm not a baby."

I counted six swear words in the time Dad and Benny had their conversation. "Why don't you get your fire alarms fixed?" Mr. Cooper yelled.

"They work just fine," Dad said. The superhero code— the code of laws all superheroes live by—demands that superheroes always tell the truth, without fail. However, we are allowed to lie to protect our identity, or when talking to supervillains, or in the name of justice. Actually, now that I think of it, the superhero code allows us to lie quite a bit.

"We're doing a fire drill," Dad continued. "You can never be too careful, especially when you have children in the house."

"You do a fire drill every month!" Mr. Cooper shouted.

"It's not rocket science. You wake up. You walk out of the house. For the love of Pete, give it a rest!"

Dad made a big deal of counting heads. "Yep, we're all safe," he said, loud enough so Mr. Cooper could hear. "And we made good time. Let's all go inside and get back to sleep."

"You don't even have all of your kids out there. And where's your wife?" Mr. Cooper yelled a few more curse words into the frigid March air, then pulled his head back in through the window.

We filed back inside, where Rodney waited for us.

"What are we looking at?" Dad asked, his voice eager.

"A citizen called the superhero line and reported a suspected robbery," Rodney said. The superhero line was a number that anybody could call to report a major crime. Rodney had written a program that listened to all the calls and sounded the alarm whenever there was a big one.

"Grandpa's made assignments," Rodney said, looking at a pad of paper in his hand. "You and Mom are going, along with four others. I'm running the video feed from downstairs."

"Wait," Benny said. "What about Rafter and me? This is going to be our first battle, right?"

Dad ignored Benny. "Where are we going? What are those villainous Johnsons trying to pull off this time?" Dad shook his fist.

"The Split Rock Museum," Rodney said. "It's just like we expected. They're making a move on the White Knight Diamond."

Dad slapped his knee. "I knew it! As soon as I read they were bringing the White Knight to town, I knew the Johnsons would try to steal it." He shook his fist. "What's that diamond worth, anyway?"

"Four-point-eight million dollars," Rodney said. "It's roughly the size of your head."

"Shooo bang!" Dad exclaimed. "That's a big diamond. That would buy those villains a whole lot of evil."

"Dad!" Benny didn't sound happy. "Why did Grandpa leave us off the list? Don't we get to go?"

In Benny's excitement to get outside, he'd forgotten his slippers. His feet were red from standing in the snow. The look on his face was one of desperation, as if all of his self-worth hinged on whether or not Dad would let him go.

"*Dad*," I said, forcefully. I tilted my head toward Benny.

Dad finally looked at us. He bent over and put his hand on Benny's shoulder. "I'm sorry, Benny," he said. "We don't have your suits ordered yet. Plus, we're working on a surprise."

"I don't want a surprise," Benny said. "I want to go to the battle. It's not fair."

"You can watch the battle on the monitors downstairs,"

Dad said. "I know how much you love that."

"I don't want to watch the battle," Benny said. "I want to *be* in the battle. Please?"

Dad hung his head and sighed. "Not this time, Benny. I really am sorry."

Benny looked like he wanted to say more, but he followed Rodney out of the kitchen.

My little brother was right. It wasn't fair. You couldn't save the day by sitting in the basement watching a screen.

I followed my brothers into the living room. Rodney went to the piano. He played the first few lines of Beethoven's Bagatelle in A Minor. A picture of dogs playing backgammon slid to the side, revealing a staircase descending to the root cellar. Rodney went down the stairs, then Benny. I was about to follow when Mom came up from the root cellar.

I've seen my parents in their supersuits at least a hundred times, but it always takes my breath away. There's something about seeing a real superhero standing just a few feet away that makes you feel like you're dreaming. Like action and adventure could explode at any time.

Our supersuits are part Kevlar, part titanium plate. We've copied the designs from the military and then we make modifications as needed. Of all the cool weapons and gadgets my family owns, I have to admit, the supersuits are my favorite. Almost all of the suits have a hydraulic system made up of pistons and heavy-duty springs. When you lift large objects, pistons kick in and give you extra strength. When you run, springs gave you superior speed. If a Johnson grabs you and tries to bend your leg backward, the titanium armor protects you.

Mom's suit is forest green and mustard yellow with black fringe—the Bailey family colors. A carbon-fiber helmet covers her head, and large goggles cover her eyes and part of her face.

I exhaled slowly as I watched Mom go through the living room toward her bedroom.

"I need to get a hair pin or I'll be fighting both the Johnsons *and* my bangs." In another moment she returned from her room. She slipped through the secret entrance and down to the root cellar. I followed.

My family goes to great pains to make sure the main and top floors of our house look normal, but the root cellar is where we can relax and be ourselves—where we can really be super.

✳

Mom met up with Dad and they strode toward the back exit. The tunnel led to some stairs and a hatch that opened out in a ravine behind our house. You can't exactly walk out your front door dressed in your supersuit.

I turned and headed toward the computer room.

My family puts cameras in their helmets to record the

battles. This allows Rodney to give direction or warning to the team. Of course, a happy side effect is that anybody who doesn't get called to go on a battle can watch it from home. Benny and I had stopped watching cartoons when we'd learned the family secret. All we did was watch past battles, over and over again.

Rodney sat in front of a bank of darkened computer monitors. He flipped a few switches on the control panel. Benny sat next to him, and I grabbed a chair on the other side.

"Okay, we're ready to roll," said Rodney. "Let's test a few things out, shall we?" His fingers flew over the keyboard as one by one the monitors came to life, a different video feed appearing on each one. He put on a headset with an attached microphone.

"Dad, can you read me?"

Dad's voice crackled over the speaker system. "I read you loud and clear. We're on our way to the museum now."

"We're all set back here at home." Rodney said. He switched off the mic and turned to Benny. "Okay, Benny, before they get to the museum, what did I tell you to remember?"

Benny rolled his eyes and let out an exaggerated sigh. "Not to stare at one monitor."

"Do you have your Benny Bag?"

Benny's face turned red. "Yes, I have my Benny Bag."

"Let's see it."

Benny held up a small brown lunch bag.

Watching a video feed from a helmet cam can make a person dizzy. I found that if I looked at different monitors, I didn't get sick, but Benny had a bad habit of staring at just one monitor until he threw up. After ruining three of Rodney's keyboards, my older brother made Benny hold a barf bag every time he watched a battle. But since Mom didn't like the word *barf*, Rodney started calling it a Benny Bag.

Dad's voice came over the speakers. "We've landed on the roof. We're going in through the elevator shaft."

I looked up at the screen and could see through Mom's camera that Dad stood on the museum's roof.

"I can open the front door if you want," Rodney said. "It's all electronic, and their security system's a joke."

"That's okay, son," Dad said. "The elevator shaft seems a little more heroic than just going in the front door."

Additional video feeds came online as more of the Baileys arrived. Dad flew to the street to pick up Uncle Ralph, Aunt Carole, and their daughter, Jessie. Jack arrived too, a stream of water shooting from his hands, allowing him to float up to the roof.

Dad accessed the elevator shaft and began flying relatives down to the first floor, where the museum kept the White Knight. In a few moments, they were all in the main room with the diamond.

"Uncle Ralph reports no sign of Johnsons," Dad said. "Jessie's going to sweep the perimeter. Aunt Carole is getting the diamond to hold for safekeeping. You've turned off the alarm, right, Rodney?"

"Finished before you even entered the building," Rodney said. "Otherwise your little elevator break-in would already have the police on their way."

I watched the monitors. The museum was so big, I had a hard time keeping track of where everybody was. "Hey, Rodney," I said. "Can you turn on the map view?"

"Coming right up," Rodney said.

One of the monitors switched to a map of the museum. Each relative showed up as a green dot. Jessie's dot patrolled the second floor while Carole's dot stood in the center of the main floor. Other dots were scattered around the building.

Okay, it's probably time I admit something. We win about half of our battles with the Johnsons. Which would be pretty good, I guess, except that we usually send out six to eight people (tonight we had six). The Johnsons *always* send four.

Four Johnsons against six or eight Baileys? It's a little embarrassing. I used to think it was because the Johnsons were better than us, but now I know they're not. I don't just watch the battles. I devour them. After three years of doing this, I've figured out their secret.

The Johnsons work together as a team. We go in with each family member doing his or her best, but we never work together. Benny and I have talked about this a lot. We agreed that when we got to go to a battle, we'd stick together. We'd help each other out. If we worked as a team, I knew we could handle anything the Johnsons threw at us.

Of course, that was before we got belly-button and polyester powers, and one more dream of mine was crushed to a mushy jam under the calloused toes of reality.

Still, one of the things I love about battles is trying to figure out the best tactics. Looking at the layout of a building or landscape and deciding how best to defend or attack? It's complicated. You have to know which powers each person has and decide where they'd be most effective.

"Look at that," I said. "There are only three ways into the diamond room, and we aren't guarding any of them. We really need to get more organized."

"What do you mean?" Benny liked hearing my ideas. "How would you do it?"

"Well, look," I said, pointing at the monitor. "You have entry points from this hall, this hall, and then the air ducts. No windows, no other doors. Air ducts are easy—you just put a guy here, and no one gets past you. Then you position two, maybe three people here. That lets you watch both halls. Three people can guard the entire space. If you wanted, the others could hide and surprise the villains when they show up."

Benny nodded. "Yeah, I think that'd work pretty well."

"But look," I said. "Jessie's up here on the second floor. They could take her by surprise and nobody would even realize it. Uncle Ralph is in the men's room . . . no, actually that's the ladies' room. And Dad—I don't know what Dad's doing—probably looking at the art. I mean, for crying out loud, the Johnsons could walk right in the front door, and it would take everybody by complete—"

A burst of static filled the computer room. My heart jumped into my throat as white noise bounced off the cement walls of the cellar.

"That's not good," Rodney said, typing some commands into the keyboard.

"—Johnsons coming in the front door," Dad said, the first part of his message cut off.

I looked at the map. Red dots poured in through the main entrance. I watched as four Johnsons raced into the museum. The dots representing Aunt Carole and Dad bumped into each other as my family tripped over themselves moving to intercept.

"See?" I said to nobody in particular. "Caught completely by surprise. And now the whole thing just becomes a chaotic free-for-all."

"Maybe so," Rodney said, grinning. "But free-for-alls are a lot of fun. There's no time for thinking during a battle!"

"Is one of those dots Juanita?" Benny said.

"I can't tell," Rodney said. "They're all moving pretty fast."

I sat transfixed in front of the monitors. I watched as the green and red dots danced and weaved around the map of the museum. I watched the live video feed, looking for tactical opportunities or errors. Nothing beats watching a battle from start to finish. It's like watching a ballet, except the costumes are cooler, and there are explosions, fighting, and large objects hurtling through the air.

"Stay out of the west wing," Rodney said. "They brought their Molten, and Jack is fighting her. The whole room is filling up with gravel."

I looked at Jack's video feed. It was just like Grandpa described. Every time the Molten Johnson sprayed lava, Jack sprayed right back with water, cooling the rock until it crumbled to gravel when it hit the ground.

"Darnedest thing I've ever seen," I said, smiling.

I heard a groan and looked over at Benny. He sat on his stool, staring at a single monitor; his head turned sideways, his eyes crossed.

"Benny, look at a different monitor!" Rodney shouted.

"My stomach feels dizzy," Benny said.

I'd seen that look before. "He's going to blow," I warned, sliding my chair backward.

Rodney waved his hands. "In the bag, Benny. In the bag!"

Benny grabbed the bag on the desk and held it up to his mouth. "Urp. Gggck."

My stomach lurched to the left a little.

"Oh, for crying out loud," Rodney said, shaking his head.

Benny pulled the bag away from his mouth.

"*Braaaaap.*" Benny's belch was loud enough to be heard over the sounds of the battle. "I didn't throw up," Benny said quickly, his face still a little green. "False alarm."

"Hang on." Rodney typed in a few commands on the keyboard. Two of the monitors went blank and then returned to life—the video feed had changed from the helmet cams to a steady view. "I just tapped into the museum's security camera system. You watch those two monitors, Benny. That should help you with your little problem."

Benny patted his stomach and smiled. "Thank you very much."

"Who's got the diamond?" I asked Rodney, looking back to the screens. It had been passed back and forth like a football.

Rodney pointed. "Uncle Ralph's got it. He's taunting their Frosty with it, see?"

Three Johnsons lunged toward Uncle Ralph, forcing him to toss the diamond to Dad, who caught it and flew into the air.

Benny gasped. "Hey, that *is* Juanita!" he said.

"Where?" I searched the screens.

"She's on monitor eight."

Dust filled the screen, giving the image a fuzzy look. But even wearing her new supersuit—complete with helmet and mask—Juanita was still recognizable. The right height. The right hair color. Even the way she moved was unmistakable.

"What's her power?" I asked.

"I haven't seen her do anything yet," Benny replied.

Juanita raised her hands—and a stream of water burst toward Dad.

Just like Jack, I thought.

"A Gusher," Benny said, his voice hushed. "That's not good."

"But not too bad," I said. Gushers can throw so much water at you it feels like a wave. Or they can shoot a stream so thin it cuts like a knife. But a power like that would be hard to use at school without everyone noticing.

Dad dodged the water, but just barely. He dropped the diamond, and it tumbled to the floor.

I'd been watching so many screens, even I was feeling a little dizzy. "Where'd the diamond go?" I asked.

"Mom's got it," Rodney replied.

I spotted the diamond, glowing blue, flying toward Mom. Juanita shot a blast of water at her, but Aunt

Carole stepped between Mom and the wave. Aunt Carole has a power similar to Great-aunt Silva Matilda's. A fireball shot out of her hand and met the liquid, turning it into a hissing cloud of steam.

"Oh, yeah," Benny said, pumping his fist. "Once we know your power, Juanita, we can handle anything you throw at—"

I stared in disbelief as Juanita turned to face Aunt Carole. A bolt of lightning erupted from her hands, narrowly missing my aunt. Aunt Carole dove for cover as a second bolt erupted over her head.

Rodney gasped. Benny looked over at me, his mouth hanging open.

"What the. . ."

We watched in stunned silence. The room flickered with light from the monitors.

Benny finally spoke.

"Juanita Johnson is a Super-super."

I couldn't believe it. I shook my head. "She can't be— that's just a myth. Isn't it, Rodney?"

A Super-super—a person with not just one superpower, but *all* the superpowers. Stories of Super-supers were just legends—like King Arthur. My family has records of superheroes that go back three hundred years, and nobody has ever had more than one power.

But unless the monitors were lying, Juanita Johnson, the girl in my algebra class, was a Super-super.

Rodney shook his head. "I don't believe it, but lightning, water . . ." His voice trailed off, his eyes never leaving the monitors. "Look at that." He pointed at a screen where Juanita hovered over two Baileys.

"She can fly, too?" Benny sounded stunned.

"This is not good," Rodney said. "Not good at all."

Someone had frozen Mom—maybe Juanita, since apparently she could do everything. Mom's hand stuck out of a wall of ice, gripping the diamond. It looked like the mother of all fancy door handles.

A Johnson plucked the diamond from Mom's hand. He turned and smiled, his lips curled up in a sneer. He began to talk, but his words didn't come over the speakers.

"Looks like he's going to start bragging and lecturing," I said. "They must think they've won."

"Look at Jessie!" Benny said. My cousin appeared over the villain's shoulder, partially hidden behind a large clay sculpture. Jessie raised her arms, and lightning crackled in a sphere between her hands.

"She's whipping up the ball lightning," Rodney said. "This is going to get good."

Someone must have warned the Johnson, because he started to turn. Before he could escape, Jessie's hands flew forward. Each of the monitors flashed a bright white, and then went black.

"She short-circuited the museum's cameras!" Rodney

said. He leaned forward and started pecking at the keyboard. "Trying to regain visual. Benny, do you need another bag?"

"No, this one's still clean."

One by one, the screens jumped back to life. It looked like my family was running. Maybe Juanita had been too much for them.

"Dad," Rodney spoke into the microphone. "What happened?"

Dad's voice came across the speakers, his voice proud. "Your cousin saved the day, that's what happened," he said. "The Johnsons have been thwarted and we return home in triumph!"

"How?" Rodney asked. "How'd you get the diamond back?"

"We didn't get it back," Dad said. "Jessie blew it up. There were too many pieces to pick up, and now we're leading the Johnsons away from the museum."

I looked at Rodney in disbelief. "Isn't blowing up the diamond a bad thing? Isn't somebody going to be really upset about that?"

Rodney shrugged. "Maybe. Probably. But at least the villains didn't get it. Maybe it's not our finest hour, but it's not a defeat. And considering we were up against a Super-super, we did pretty good."

There was nothing else to do. Benny wanted to stay

up and wait for Mom and Dad, but I went upstairs and crawled into bed.

In the darkness of the room, my breathing came faster. Benny and I weren't just facing a supervillain— but a super-supervillain. If it was really true, we'd have to deal with invisibility, lighting, fire, strength . . .

I wanted to jump out of bed, put on my shoes, and run away. Maybe Benny and I could leave the city and go to a different school. Or maybe we could move in with Grandpa. I'd like to think I was afraid not because I was a coward, but because I had brains. Going back to school was crazy. It was insane.

Iron resolve. Ferocious courage. And a healthy dose of insanity.

I realized I had the covers over my head. That's not how a superhero acted. Angry, I pushed aside the covers. A superhero faced challenges. He didn't run.

I closed my eyes, and that seemed to help clear my mind. I'd stared at the map of the museum for so long the dots seemed to float in the darkness behind my eyelids.

An idea hit me—a crazy idea.

I got out of bed and went to my desk. I pulled out a piece of paper and made a quick sketch of my school, drawing it like a blueprint. I marked the important rooms, the ones involved in the plan—my algebra class, the lunchroom, the library.

I finished the drawing and stared at it.

Benny came in from downstairs. "What are you doing?"

When I spoke, I could hear the excitement in my voice. "Benny, I think I've solved our Juanita problems."

"Really?" Benny said. "How?"

I smiled. "We'll do the last thing Juanita would expect."

"What's that?" Benny's asked.

"We're going on the offensive," I said. "We're going to take the fight to Juanita, and we're going to get our real powers."

Benny grinned in the darkness. "Now you're talking like a superhero."

6

I WISH I'D BROUGHT A PAIR OF SUSPENDERS

I worked on the plan until I fell asleep. I wrote it out step by step the next morning over breakfast. When Benny and I got on the bus, we sat close to the front. Not close enough that the bus driver could hear us, but close enough that Juanita wouldn't try anything.

Juanita had missed one day, and I secretly hoped she'd miss another. It would give me time to perfect my plan. But when the bus pulled up to the curb at Juanita's stop, she was standing there.

I felt a twinge of the terror I'd felt the previous night, but I remembered Grandpa's words. I took a few deep breaths, and that helped. Or maybe it just made me light-headed.

The door opened, and Juanita Johnson—a Super-supervillain—climbed onto the bus. Her slim frame made her look almost frail. She had olive skin and dark curly hair. Her brown eyes could twinkle and dance when she talked with a friend, and then turn to daggers when she looked at me or Benny.

I glanced casually out the window, trying to appear disinterested, pretending I didn't know that she could turn invisible, or shock me, or pick me up and throw me out the window of the bus.

I took another deep breath.

"Stay calm," I whispered to Benny, although he already looked completely calm. Juanita made her way through the sea of green seats toward us. "She's coming this way."

"Well, when you think about it, it's the only way she can come," Benny said. "It's not like the bus is a maze or anything."

Juanita walked past, and for a moment, I thought she'd ignore us. But then she was there, leaning right over my shoulder. She said four words in a voice that was low and dripping with venom. Four words that sent a chill through my stomach.

"Go ahead. Try it."

And then she was gone.

For a moment I thought she'd disappeared—that she'd used her superpowers to vanish. I braced for an attack.

Nothing happened.

I stole a glance over my shoulder. Juanita sat alone at the back of the bus. She stared out the window.

Benny whispered in my ear. "For somebody who just got every power in the book, she doesn't look very happy."

"She's a Johnson," I said, shaking my fist. Then I lowered my voice. "Villains are never happy."

I faced forward in my seat. "Are you ready?" I asked.

"Ready for what?" Benny asked.

"I've got a plan," I said. "We're going to find out how the Johnsons took our powers."

Benny grinned. "Let's do it right now. Here, on the bus."

I shook my head. "Not on the bus. We wouldn't be able to talk. The trick is to be in a public place without anybody being able to overhear. Let me show you." I pulled out my notes and map of the school, spreading them out on my leg. "Okay, at lunch, you and I will meet up here at the library. Got it?"

"Why the library?" Benny asked.

"The library is right next to the cafeteria," I explained. "Nobody hangs out in the library, but the librarian will be there, and that should be enough to keep Juanita from attacking, but still allow us to talk to her in private."

Benny nodded, "But how do we get Juanita to the library?"

"Rodney has all of the Johnsons' phone numbers. We're going to hide over here, deep in the stacks," I pointed to the section of my map that had all of the bookcases. "Once we're in place, I'll tell Rodney to send a text message to Juanita. He'll tell her to go to the library. He said he can mask it so she won't see who it's from. Once she's in the library, we'll confront her and find out how her family stole our powers. Does that make sense?"

"Got it," Benny said. "Although I wish I'd brought a pair of suspenders."

"Suspenders? Benny . . . what are you talking about?"

"I have a hard time talking to girls," Benny said. "I never know what to do with my hands. If I had suspenders, I could hook my thumbs under the straps."

"Juanita's not a girl," I said. "She's a supervillain."

I went over the plan again, just to be sure. When the bus stopped in front of our school, we piled off the bus. Benny and I spent a few minutes standing in the snow outside the front doors in full view of at least a dozen kids. Juanita got off the bus, and without giving Benny or me a second glance, she walked inside.

The bell rang, so we split up. My first class, history, usually crawled by. All my teacher did was stand in front of the class and tell us how miserable life was at certain points in history. He'd say things like, "You think cleaning the toilet is rough? Try emptying a chamber pot." But on that day, history was over before I knew it. The bell rang, and I had to leave.

I paused at the door outside algebra. Juanita sat at her desk, her back toward me—waiting.

My teacher was nowhere in sight. That was strange.

"I believe you're late," a voice said behind me.

I turned and had to look up. Way up. A tall, slim man with a balding head and a bow tie towered over me. The man was old, probably sixty or more. He hunched over a little, reminding me of a gorilla.

"Uh," I said. "My teacher isn't here yet. I was just going in."

"Your teacher is here," said gorilla man. "I'm your new teacher. Your old teacher has . . . let's just say he found other things with which to occupy his time."

Something wasn't right. I went in and sat at my desk. The man walked to the front of the class.

Juanita turned in her seat and stared at me. I couldn't read her face. She looked at me as if she were waiting for something. I returned her gaze until she finally turned back to the front of the classroom.

I felt dizzy.

The new teacher picked up a ruler and a piece of chalk. He slapped the ruler against the desktop with a crack. "Quiet, class." His voice was loud and clear. "I'll be your teacher for the rest of the year. Mr. Richter won't be back. Allow me to introduce myself."

The teacher went to the board and wrote his name. I felt my throat tighten.

Every time I thought things couldn't sink any lower, the universe seemed to slap me upside the head and say, "You ain't seen nothing yet, buster."

The man turned and looked directly at me. "My name is Nicholas. But you can call me Mr. Johnson."

7

WATCH THIS

I met Benny outside his class right as lunch began. Students poured out of rooms, pushing and shoving their way into the halls. We fought through the crowd, making our way toward the library. In the chaos, I could talk to Benny in relative privacy.

"We've got to move fast." I told Benny about the new teacher. "There are now two Johnsons, right here inside the school, and one of them is a you-know-what." A *Super-super* is what I wanted to say, but couldn't. I shook my fist.

Benny raised his eyebrows. "Will you have to shake your fist every time you talk to your teacher? And what about parent-teacher conferences? Holy cow, that's going to be awkward."

We got to the library. I stepped inside and pulled out my phone to text Rodney. *Send Juanita.*

I was about to hit send when I happened to glance up.

Sitting at a table toward the back of the library, with her feet on the table, was Juanita Johnson. She was reading a book.

I lurched to a stop and Benny crashed into me. I didn't have time to think. I grabbed Benny by the sleeve and ducked behind a book cart off to my left. I fell to the ground, pulling Benny down next to me.

My brother crouched on his hands and knees, looking at me in alarm. "What is it? Why did you—"

I put a finger to my lips and Benny fell silent. I raised my head, peeking around the corner of the cart. Juanita was totally engrossed in her book. I didn't think she'd seen us. Scanning the room, I could see Mr. Wells in his office eating lunch, but there was no sign of anyone else.

Juanita looked up and I dropped back behind the cart.

Benny mouthed the words, *what's going on?*

I motioned toward where Juanita was sitting and mouthed her name.

Benny peeked around the cart and whispered, "So? Isn't the whole plan to talk with her and find out what the Johnsons did to our powers?" He shook his fist.

"But she shouldn't be here," I said. "I was counting on surprising her. Rodney was going to send her a text, but it's like she knew exactly what—"

And then it hit me. I smacked my forehead. "I'm so dumb."

"What?" Benny asked.

"We talked about our plan on the bus."

"You're not making any sense." Benny said.

"Juanita is a Super-super," I explained. "That means she has super hearing. She probably sat in the back of the bus and heard every word we said. If she knows our plan, we could be walking right into a trap."

"A trap?" Benny said. "In the library? What kind of trap can you set in a library? What's she going to do, throw an *I love to read* poster at us?"

My brother had a point. As long as Mr. Wells was watching, she wouldn't be able to use her powers against us.

"This wasn't part of the original plan," I said.

Benny shrugged. "We'll wing it."

Wing it. I took a deep breath. "Okay. Get ready." I stood up.

Juanita was gone.

Benny got up and looked around. "Well, that's a little strange," he muttered.

In front of us was an open area. Tables where students could read dotted the floor. The only way Juanita could have gotten past us was to walk through the door behind us. There was a desk to one side of the door where Mr.

Wells checked out books.

That left one other place.

"She must have gone back into the stacks," Benny said.

To our right, a large bookshelf divided the open area and the stacks. Our library is a little different from most other schools. One of the parents in the school district made a lot of money selling mechanical bookcases to big universities and public libraries. When they remodeled our school about five years ago, the parent donated one of these systems. The bookshelves are mostly crammed together, with just a few aisles in between. When you press a button on the side of the bookcases, the aisle in front of you opens up, and somewhere else the bookcases close. The good news is, this allows you to pack more books into a smaller place. The bad news is, a supervillain can use this to her advantage.

"Uh, Benny?" I said.

"Yeah?"

"I think I just realized how Juanita could spring a trap." I pointed to the area of the library into which Juanita had disappeared. "With one press of a button, she could smash us flat."

Benny shook his head. "That's not how it works. There's a safety mechanism that keeps that from happening. If somebody is in an aisle then the bookcases don't close."

"Benny, Juanita has *all* the powers. How long do you

think it would take Rodney to disable that safety mechanism?" I asked.

Benny looked over at me. He opened his mouth but nothing came out. Then he finally spoke. "That's not so good."

I hesitated. We were still standing close enough to the door that we could run away. Students were walking through the halls on the way to the cafeteria. Juanita might not dare to attack us in the open, but if we went back into the stacks, we'd be out of sight—of both the students and Mr. Wells.

Benny saw my hesitation. "Rafter," he said. "If we don't face Juanita now, we'll be afraid every single day for the rest of our lives. This is what being super is all about."

I wondered if this was the ferocious courage Grandpa talked about, or if it was the healthy dose of insanity.

Maybe it was a little of both.

"Stay close," I said. "We'll go into the stacks just long enough to lead Juanita back out here into the open area, got it?"

Benny nodded.

A long bookcase stood before us. On the left was a walkway leading back into the stacks. A large mural of Split Rock was painted on the wall. On the right was another walkway, also leading into the stacks.

I walked slowly down the walkway to the left. I kept my eyes trained right, searching for Juanita. When we reached the back wall we still hadn't seen her.

"Where did she go?" Benny asked.

"She must be hiding on the other side," I whispered. "Either that, or she's invisible."

We stood in the corner of the stacks, with the mural behind us. I felt more than a little claustrophobic. We could scoot to the other walkway, but that meant walking between a bookcase and a solid brick wall. Juanita would be able to close the shelves on us.

"It's like being stuck between a rock and a bookcase." Benny was trying to be funny, but his voice sounded nervous.

I took a step into the aisle. There were about three feet between the brick wall to my left and the bookcase to my right. The shelves didn't move fast, but Juanita might have modified that as well. The bookcase loomed like a wave waiting to crash over us.

I took another step. And then another.

We were halfway back down the aisle when I heard Juanita's voice pierce the quiet library.

"Show me what you've got, villains. Make your move."

I stopped dead in my tracks. My brain couldn't register what she'd just said.

Benny spoke from behind me, calling into the shelves. "Who in the heck are you talking to?"

Again Juanita's voice floated through the library. It hissed in my ear. "To the only villains in this school.

Rafter and Benny Bailey."

I heard what sounded like a spitting noise.

Benny twirled his finger around his ear and mouthed the word *cuckoo*.

"We're not villains." I felt like an idiot for stating such an obvious fact. I also felt like an idiot talking to a bunch of books on a shelf.

My words were met with a burst of laughter. "Right. Not villains. You boys must think I'm a moron."

"Now that's the first thing you've said that makes sense," Benny said.

The floor began vibrating under my feet. The shelves were moving. Aunt Verna once told me that a little bit of knowledge never hurt anybody. But Aunt Verna had never been trapped in the stacks with a Super-super. We were about to be *crushed* by knowledge.

I spun on my heels and pushed Benny back toward the mural and to safety. I couldn't be sure the bookcase was closing in on us, but when we got to the end and I turned around, I saw the stack slowly close against the brick wall. At least Juanita hadn't adjusted the speed.

"That is a serious misuse of school property," Benny said, shaking his head.

My goal had been to lead Juanita into the open area, but now I was mad. "Come on." I spoke so that only Benny could hear. "We're done being pushed around."

I walked past several bookcases until I came to an open aisle. I took a few steps in and then bent over, peering between the books on the shelves. I saw a pair of jeans among the stacks. Juanita was two aisles in front of me, walking carefully toward the mural. I stood up and moved in the opposite direction. I wanted to circle around and come up behind her. Benny followed.

"Lie all you want," I said loud enough for Juanita to hear me. "The Baileys are the upholders of truth and justice in Split Rock."

"So you Baileys decided to destroy the White Knight Diamond in the name of truth and justice?" There was another spitting sound.

"No, we kept you from stealing it." I got to the end of the aisle, turned right around the corner, and entered the aisle where I'd seen the jeans. Juanita was crouched down, looking between the shelves. I wondered why she wasn't using her X-ray vision. When she spotted me, she stood up straight, knowing she'd been caught. Her face flushed, and for a moment I thought she looked . . . uncertain. Then she scowled and folded her arms across her chest, her dark curly hair falling over both shoulders.

Juanita Johnson did not look nice. I could almost imagine fire or lasers or lava shooting out of her eyes. I had to will my feet to stand firm. Benny came and stood next to me, and that helped.

"Oh, that's a good one," Juanita said. "Break into a museum, destroy a national treasure, and then try to blame it on us?

"Your family is *always* involved in evil plans," she continued. "Like the battle last fall when you tried building the giant laser in the thermal underwear factory."

"A laser? In a thermal underwear factory? Can you even hear how crazy you sound? Why would anybody do that?"

"Because you Baileys are all crazy." Juanita turned her head and spit. There was a garbage can in the general direction she turned, but I doubted she could be that accurate.

"That's just like vandalism," Benny said. "You might as well spray-paint the mural."

I wondered how I could get Juanita back out in the open, and then realized I could beat her at her own game. I reached up and pressed the button on the side of the bookcase. The grinding under our feet resumed as the stacks began to slide.

I ran toward the open area of the library with Benny on my heels.

I cleared the end of the stacks and froze.

Mr. Wells sat at his desk, talking to my new teacher.

Mr. Johnson.

Back into the stacks. This game of cat and mouse was getting intense—there were too many cats.

To leave the library we'd have to walk right past a supervillain. But if we kept running around inside the stacks we risked bumping into a *Super*-supervillain.

We couldn't go left or right. We couldn't go forward or back. That left only one option.

Up.

Finding an open aisle, I placed my foot on the lowest shelf, testing its strength.

I climbed hand over hand until I got to the top of the shelf. Crawling on top of the bookcase, I turned around and motioned for Benny to come up. He started to climb.

Benny was almost to the top when I heard the familiar rumble and looked down. The bookcases were closing in on him.

"Benny," I whispered. "Give me your hand."

"I can't." Benny clung to the bookcase. "If I give you my hand, I'll fall."

Oh no! I'd forgotten Benny didn't like heights. But there was no time to argue. Lying flat on my stomach, I grabbed the opposite side of the shelf with one hand, and then reached down with the other and grabbed Benny's belt. I pulled hard, hauling him up out of the aisle. The stacks closed together, just missing his right leg.

Benny and I lay flat on the shelves. My brother gasped and hung on for dear life.

"You just gave me the mother of all wedgies," he said.

"And I can't even let go to straighten things up."

I got to my feet, crouching low so I wouldn't be seen by Mr. Wells or Mr. Johnson at the front of the library. Juanita had to be farther back into the stacks, which meant there was now a gaping chasm between her and me. I looked down. The carpet didn't look that soft. And if I was caught jumping on top of the bookcases . . . somehow I didn't think Mr. Wells would be too happy about that.

But I was a superhero. Risk was just part of the job description. I spit into my hands and wiped them on the bottom of my shoes. I didn't want to slip on the dusty bookcases. I stepped to the edge of the shelves, bent over, and jumped.

As soon as I was airborne, I heard the bookcases rumble.

My instincts took over. The shelf I was jumping to was sliding forward and now I was headed toward empty space.

I collided with the side of the shelf, unable to stop. But I pushed myself off almost as soon as I touched it. Instead of falling into the new aisle that was opening up, I went farther than I'd meant to and landed on the top of a group of bookshelves, rolling onto my side. Luckily there were five shelves pressed together, and I had time to bring myself to a stop.

Benny was still hanging on to the top of the first

bookcase for dear life, but he managed to give me a thumbs-up and a grin.

I pointed to my eyes with two fingers, and then to Benny. I motioned in the direction of Mr. Wells and Mr. Johnson. I wanted Benny to watch and give me some kind of signal if either of them moved. Benny nodded and scooted to where he could watch. I only hoped that he understood.

I was covered in thick dust and felt a scratch in my throat. I resisted the urge to cough as I crawled over the top of the bookcases. Finally, I came to the next open aisle and looked down. Juanita crouched below, peering between shelves. She was hunting us all right. But why wasn't she using her super hearing? Or speed?

Maybe I could be a little more bold.

I thought back to what she'd said about the battle at the thermal underwear factory. I remembered that battle.

Swinging my feet over the bookcase, I took a deep breath, pushed off, and dropped to the floor. I landed two feet from Juanita and was rewarded with a look of alarm. Juanita stumbled and fell, landing on her rear end. She scooted back on her hands and feet.

I spoke calmly to show I was in complete control. "We got a call from a citizen telling us you were smuggling illegal weapons into the country." Juanita scrambled to her feet, glaring at me. I kept right on talking. "And *your* family was storing them in that factory. That was one of our greatest battles ever. We beat you even though we were down by three people because Uncle Ralph and his family all had dental appointments."

I don't know what I was expecting. Maybe for Juanita to attack. Or for her to keep telling lies. I was ready for anything . . . except what happened next.

Juanita softened. The anger in her face diminished and turned into confusion.

"We weren't smuggling weapons," she said.

"What are you talking about?"

"The thermal underwear factory." Juanita looked like she was trying to read my mind. "*We* got a call from a citizen warning us that you were building a laser. *We* saved the day by destroying the machinery."

I shook my head. "No. I'm pretty sure that machinery was what they used to make thermal underwear."

Juanita got to the end of the aisle. "Don't try to confuse me, Rafter Bailey." She turned her head and made a spitting noise. This time I thought I heard something hit the plastic lining of a garbage can.

Juanita pointed at her chest with a thumb. "*We* are the superheroes. *You* are the villains."

She reached over to the shelf and pressed the button.

I was still in the middle of the aisle, no time to reach either end. I jumped back on the shelves and started to climb. The bookcases were closing together. I got to the top just as the shelves slammed shut under me.

I signaled to Benny to let him know I was okay.

He was waving his arms furiously, pointing toward the wall on my left. I looked over and saw the top of a head, bobbing between the bookshelves.

A new voice penetrated the stacks of the library. "Juanita? Are you back here?"

Mr. Johnson. I lay down on the top of the bookshelf, trying to make myself as flat as possible.

"I'm over here, Uncle Nicholas."

Mr. Johnson found Juanita. "Are you okay? I looked for you after lunch." Mr. Johnson didn't sound like a supervillain. He sounded like a concerned uncle.

All Juanita had to do was tell her uncle where we were. There was no escape.

Juanita was silent for several moments. Then she spoke. "I'm fine."

What? Why wasn't she telling on us?

"All right," Mr. Johnson said. "I need to get back to class. I'll see you after school."

"Thanks, Uncle Nicholas."

I watched Mr. Johnson's bobbing head until it left the stacks. Juanita walked out just behind him, turning back only once to glance over her shoulder. Our eyes met, but I couldn't read her.

I got to my feet, perching like a gargoyle on top of the library bookcase.

What was going on?

Benny wobbled to his feet, trying to mimic my actions despite his fear of heights. He licked his hands, and wiped them on his feet. He jumped over the open aisle and then came and sat next to me.

"What was all that about?" he whispered. "What happened?"

Before I could admit I had no idea, I saw a bald head turn the corner and reenter the stacks.

Mr. Johnson had doubled back into the library.

"Get down," I whispered to Benny.

I dropped to my stomach. The library was quiet enough that I could hear his footsteps along the side of the stacks. After a moment he stopped.

"I am here at this school to protect my niece." Mr. Johnson's voice was flat. "She is important to me. I will not be very nice to anyone who tries to hurt her."

Mr. Johnson was moving again. Benny opened his mouth, but I shook my head sharply to silence him. But Benny couldn't control it—he looked like he was about to sneeze.

I waved my hands, trying to get him to stop, but there really wasn't any point. Benny curled up on top of the shelves and sneezed. A puff of dust blew into the air.

I froze in terror. I was certain that Mr. Johnson would find us now. There was a horrible pause, and then the shelves started to move once again.

Benny scrambled, afraid. His leg slipped over the edge of the shelf just as the bookcase he was on started moving against the back wall. If Benny couldn't pull himself up, he'd be crushed.

I leaned over to grab Benny's arms, but in doing so I slipped, too. For a brief moment, Benny and I held on to each other, a bookcase between us, our feet dangling in midair. I could see the wall getting closer and closer.

"Rafter, help!"

My grip gave out. I crashed down into the open aisle, landing on my feet, but ramming my shoulder against a shelf. I raced down the aisle and moved to the back wall, terrified at what I would find.

What I saw was my brother, his hands on the top shelf of the bookcase, and his feet pressing against the wall behind him. I watched in amazement as he began to push the bookcase back.

He looked heroic. He looked super. He was almost horizontal to the ground, keeping who knows how many bookcases from crushing him.

But while Benny was pushing the top of the stack back, the bottom of the stack was still moving forward. I watched in horror as books began to slide off the shelves.

The bookcase started to lean until I was sure it would fall.

A sharp crack pierced the library. It sounded like a tree branch snapping in two.

"Uh-oh," I heard Benny say, and then he and the shelf went crashing to the ground.

There was another crack as the first shelf tipped into the second one. And then a third and a fourth. Like dominoes, the shelves began tumbling over, books flying everywhere. Dust flew into the air and a wave of sound reverberated around the room.

From his office, Mr. Wells shouted, "MY LIBRARY!"

Benny staggered to his feet, tripping over books and shaking dust from his shirt.

He looked up at me and I knew there was only one sensible thing to do.

Run.

I sprinted toward the far side of the stacks, keeping low behind the toppled mounds of broken bookcases and books. Benny followed.

Students were pouring into the library from the halls. Mr. Wells was yelling at everybody to stay back, but in just a few seconds the library was filled with kids trying to see what had happened. As soon as we were surrounded by students, Benny and I stealthily slipped out and into the hall. We walked quickly to the nearest exit and then pushed out into the cold afternoon sun.

And then we were running—our feet kicking up wet snow—racing along the wall of the school.

"Did you see that?" Benny said. "Did you see what I did to the library?"

"I saw." I turned the corner of the school and skidded to a stop next to some bushes. "Let's just hope nobody else did."

I put my hands on my knees and breathed hard. We'd made it. We'd come face to face with a Super-super and still we'd made it.

We were safe.

And then I heard feet crunching in the snow, and before I could move, Juanita was upon us.

8.

WE DON'T EVEN HAVE A TACO NIGHT

Juanita grabbed us both by our collars. She might have looked small and fragile, but in an instant she took two short steps and threw us into the bushes. I expected to be stopped by limbs and branches, but instead I fell through the foliage into an opening between the bushes and the wall of the school.

Juanita had us trapped.

I turned my back against the wall, bracing for her attack.

Juanita crouched on her hands and knees. I could see white mist escaping from her mouth as she panted.

"What were you saying in there about not being

villains?" Her voice sounded sarcastic. "And remind me, who just destroyed the school library?"

I opened my mouth, but nothing came out.

Benny jumped to my rescue. "Well, we wouldn't have had to destroy it if you hadn't tried to smash us."

Juanita glared.

In a much smaller voice, Benny said, "Do you think Mr. Wells is going to be mad?"

"Oh, I think everybody is going to be mad, Bailey," Juanita said. "The only reason I don't turn you in right now is because it might give away my secret identity." Juanita turned her head and spit.

"Does your mouth ever dry out with all that spitting you do?" I asked.

Juanita didn't bother answering.

"We'll probably have to tell the librarian," Benny said. Clearly Juanita's mind games were working. "That would be the right thing to do."

"We were defending the school from a villain," I said, looking directly at Juanita. "We can't tell the librarian without explaining that we're superheroes."

"Supervillains," Juanita said.

"Superheroes."

"*Supervillains.*"

"Superheroes!"

"SUPERVIL—"

"Can I say something?" Benny asked.

Juanita shrugged. "I'm not your teacher. You can talk whenever you want."

Benny cleared his throat. "I got my superpower on Monday. And it's worthless."

I looked over at my brother in horror.

Juanita's face went dark. Her eyes narrowed, and for a moment she looked like a snake about to strike. "What did you just say?"

"He didn't say anything. Benny, don't say another word."

Benny, of course, went right on talking. "My power lets me turn my belly button from an innie to an outie." He got on his knees and lifted his shirt. With a soft pop his belly button became an outie. Another pop and it became an innie. "That's my superpower."

I couldn't help it. I slapped myself on the forehead. Now Juanita knew we were powerless. Or rather, that Benny was powerless. I could still try to bluff.

"If you try to hurt him," I said, doing my best to sound threatening, "my power is"—I realized I should've thought of a fake power earlier—"uh, I can shoot microwaves out of my eyes."

Benny looked surprised. "Microwaves? Wouldn't that hurt when they came out? They're all big and square."

"Not the appliances, Benny," I said. "Just the waves.

You know . . . like on taco night. When I melted all that cheese for your nachos with my eyes."

"We don't even have a taco night."

I couldn't read Juanita's face. She looked at Benny for a long time. Her face seemed to soften, and I realized for the first time that when she wasn't scowling or spitting, Juanita looked almost pretty.

When she finally spoke, her voice was quiet. "That was very brave of you, Benny Bailey." Almost as an afterthought, she turned her head and spit.

"Thank you," Benny said, and then before I could stop him: "Rafter's real power is that he can light matches on polyester."

"Benny!"

Juanita looked from Benny to me. Her face softened a little more. "I got a worthless power too."

At last I'd caught her in a lie. "We saw you," I said. "At the museum. You have all those powers."

"My aunt is a Light Shifter," Juanita said. "Do you have one of those?"

Benny nodded. "We have a cousin in Oak City who's a Light Shifter. She bends light and can make herself look like anybody she wants. And she can disguise people who are nearby too. One time for Halloween, she gave me a mustache and an extra set of armpits so I could—"

"Benny," I said. "Not now."

Juanita continued. "My aunt went to the museum and made it appear as if I was there. She took turns making each person look like me. I was at home in bed. We did it to confuse your family. That's also why my uncle came to teach our algebra class. To protect me from you two."

My mind was spinning. She had to be lying. "The bookcases," I said. "They were closing in on us. How did you disable the safety mechanism?"

Juanita looked at me like I was crazy. "I didn't disable anything. The shelves only close when there's no one standing on the ground. If you two wouldn't have started climbing shelves like monkeys, you wouldn't have had any problems."

I felt more than a little silly. I had a million questions, but I ended up asking only one. "If you're not a Super-super," I asked, "what is your power?"

Juanita leaned toward me. Our noses were almost touching, and I could feel her breath on my face. I smelled ginger and cinnamon.

An electronic buzzer cut through the cold air. I couldn't help but jump.

"Lunch is over," Juanita said. "I have to go to P.E."

And with that, Juanita Johnson turned and crawled out of the bushes.

9

GET THE TRIPLE MEAT OR
GET NOTHING

The principal called a meeting in the gym with the entire school. He demanded to know who had caused the destruction to the library. Benny and I could say nothing without giving away our identities. I saw Juanita sitting several bleachers down, her face pointing forward. She never looked at anyone. Finally, we were sent back to class.

Benny and I didn't get a chance to talk until after school. I got off the bus and followed him to our room, where he immediately grabbed a comic book and flopped down on his bed.

"Benny," I said. "Why did you tell Juanita your power?"

"We're superheroes," he shrugged. "We don't lie."

"The superhero code lets us lie to villains," I reminded him.

"Yeah, I know, but still . . ." He put the comic book down. "I felt like we could handle anything she threw at us the honest way. We didn't need to lie about our powers."

I raised my eyebrows. "You thought that you and I could stand up to a Super-super? With your belly-button trick, and my polyester power? I didn't even have any matches."

"It's not a trick," Benny said. "It's a power. And we did stand up to her. I'm pretty sure we won that battle."

"I don't know about that," I said. "But I'm pretty sure the library lost."

Benny got off the bed and started his push-up routine.

"How many are you up to?" I asked.

"Eleven," Benny grunted as he struggled to lift his frame off the carpet.

I counted as Benny did eleven push-ups, and then one more.

"*Twelve!*" Benny said, collapsing to the floor, and then rising to a kneeling position. "At this rate, I'll be up to a thousand by June."

"Do you really think Juanita got a worthless power?" I asked.

"Maybe," Benny said. "Her story about the Light Shifter makes sense."

"None of it makes sense to me," I said, rubbing my forehead.

Dad poked his head into the room. "Ah, Rafter. There you are. How would you like to go on patrol with me tonight?"

Patrol is just what it sounds like. Every night, one of the Baileys goes out into the city looking for evildoers—citizens committing crimes. With a million people in Split Rock, you'd think patrol would mean a night of action and adventure.

It doesn't. The citizens of Split Rock know that super-heroes roam the city, so they tend to be on their best behavior. Frankly, patrol is boring, but after talking to Juanita, I had a few questions for Dad. "Okay," I said. "Right after dinner?"

"Yep," Dad said. "Eat hearty and dress warm. Tonight we battle with criminals."

After dinner I changed into my patrol clothes. I pulled on some thermal underwear and then a pair of black jeans and a black hoodie. I wouldn't need any of this when I got my supersuit. I grabbed a ski mask and my phone and headed downstairs.

Dad was waiting for me in the root cellar. He no longer looked like the skinny guy who wore a pocket protector and bow tie to the office. He wore his supersuit. The titanium plates were molded to look like bulging muscles. His green and yellow costume was clean and wrinkle free. He looked heroic. He looked super. If you were a bad guy, you wouldn't want to meet him in a dark alley.

Dad and I followed the tunnel to the back exit. I climbed up a ladder and opened a hatch. A few small trees and some brush provided cover, and we slipped into the night without anybody noticing.

The air was cold, and the stars shivered in the night sky. "Are you ready?" Dad asked, and without waiting for an answer, he grabbed me around the waist and leaped into the dark.

I love to fly. Not the kind of flying that's done in a plane or a helicopter—the real kind of flying, when there's nothing between you and the whole world. It's something I'll never grow tired of.

I watched the earth fall away under my feet. Dad held me tight, and even thousands of feet up I felt safe. The worries and cares of the past two days seemed to fade into the background.

The frigid air bit at my face, so I put on the ski mask.

"Where are we going tonight?" I asked, yelling to be heard over the rushing wind.

"Wherever there is danger!" Dad declared in his booming superhero voice.

I could tell Dad secretly wished for a crime wave—something to make patrol a bit more exciting. But Split Rock had been in a solid obedience wave for years.

"Let's go downtown," Dad said. "By the public library.

You never know what wild and crazy things might be happening at the library."

I remembered the shelves and books and dust crashing around the school library. "Uh . . . right, Dad."

Dad flew toward a group of skyscrapers. He soared in between buildings and around them. I held out my hands and felt the wind bite at my fingers.

Nothing was happening at the library. Or the City Center. Or the taco shack next to the City Center. Dad was about to fly to his favorite tire store when he pulled up short.

"What have we here?"

I looked to where Dad was pointing. "A guy crossing the street?"

"Exactly," Dad replied. "And look where he's doing it—right in the middle of the block! That, my son, is called *jaywalking*. And we caught him red-handed—or red-footed, as the case may be."

Dad deposited me on the limb of a tree. "You wait here. Oh, and take this." He pulled a small camera out of his utility belt. "If I look particularly heroic, snap a picture for the family website."

He floated down to the man who, by this time, was getting into his car. I watched Dad pick him up, carry him halfway down the block, and drop him gently onto a crosswalk.

"No need to thank me," Dad called as he flew away. I couldn't hear what the man was yelling, but it didn't sound like he was shouting his thanks.

"That guy was almost in his car," I said when Dad returned to the tree. "Now he has to walk all the way around."

"Yes," Dad said. "But now he's obeying the law, and he'll be able to sleep better because of it." Dad took the camera back from me. "How did I look? Did you get a picture?"

"No," I said. "It was too dark. Sorry." We spent the next two hours flying around looking for murderers, thieves, or perhaps another jaywalker. We found nothing.

Dad finally stationed us on top of a bank. I think he was hoping for a good old-fashioned robber to drop in and attempt a grand heist. Sometime around nine o'clock the temperature dropped below freezing, and I started shivering.

"I can take you back home if you want," Dad offered. "I feel bad. My supersuit keeps me nice and toasty."

"I'm okay," I said.

I decided it was time to talk. I didn't know exactly how to bring up the subject, so I did it in a roundabout way.

"So, what did the news have to say about the diamond heist?" I asked.

Dad shrugged. "If you read the right news, they condemned the actions of the Johnsons and praised us for saving the day."

"And what did the wrong news say?" I asked.

"Something about destroying a national treasure," Dad said. "Which I do feel bad about. Maybe Jessie got a little overexcited with her lightning. But still . . . the Johnsons would have stolen the diamond if we hadn't stepped in. And who knows what evil purpose they would have used it for?"

"Didn't we kind of mess things up?" I asked Dad.

"Well, I guess that's one way of describing it." Dad looked thoughtful. "It certainly wasn't a battle we'll highlight at the reunion. But think about it, before we got to that museum, they only had one huge diamond, and it cost millions of dollars to own. Even if you can afford it, what are you going to do with it? You can't exactly make an earring out of it. The weight would tear your ear clean off. Now, they have lots of little diamonds that won't tear anybody's ears off."

Dad's explanation wasn't helping my confusion. "Dad, have you ever wondered . . . I mean . . . what if the Johnsons aren't evil? What if they think *they* are superheroes, just like us?" I shook my fist, but only barely.

Dad looked over at me. I expected him to laugh—or to tell me that I was crazy—but he didn't. "You're growing up faster than I like," Dad said.

"What are you talking about?"

"I remember having this same talk with your grandpa," Dad said. "It's part of becoming a superhero."

I still didn't follow. Dad finally continued.

"You have to remember, son, that supervillains are

masters of deception. In comic books the bad guy is easy to spot because he wears a black costume and has an evil-sounding name. Like Lord Agony or Mr. Meany Pants. In the real world, things aren't so obvious. The Johnsons"—Dad shook his fist—"spend a very large portion of their time spreading lies about us to the good citizens of Split Rock. All you have to do is read the wrong newspaper or the wrong blog and you'll find people who have been tricked. It's all part of the supervillainy, and they're very good at it."

I remembered Juanita's face in the library. "Juanita told me she got a worthless power too. I don't think she was lying. At least not about that."

"She's a supervillain," Dad said. "She's probably been taking lying lessons since she was three."

"Lying lessons?"

"Yeah, from her family," Dad said. "Or maybe from the internet. You can find anything on the internet. I once found a video that taught you how to tap-dance the Canadian national anthem in Morse code."

I didn't think Juanita had been taking lying lessons on the internet, but Dad did have a good point. If the Johnsons were villains, of course they'd be good at lying. And deceiving.

But why? What were they up to?

"The important thing is this," Dad said. "All your

life your mom and I have taught you that the Johnsons are villains. And it's true. They are. But now you need to discover that for yourself. You can't take my word for it. If you're going to spend the *rest* of your life fighting the Johnsons, then you need to find out for yourself."

"How do I do that?" I asked.

"Well," Dad said. "When I was your age, I read the newspapers. I went to the library and looked up books. You can probably do the same thing on Google. I'm convinced that when you look at the big picture, you'll come to the same conclusion."

I looked down to the street below. The wind blew a few scraps of paper and leaves through the deserted street. I thought it strange that a place could be so busy and loud during the day, but so peaceful and still at night.

And that's when I saw it out of the corner of my eye—a glint of light—down in the drugstore across from the bank. At first I wondered if I'd seen anything. . . . But there in the darkness of the store, I saw it again—the small flicker of a flashlight.

"Dad," I said, pointing. "There's something going on down there."

"What?" Dad sounded excited. "Where? Is somebody doing something evil?"

"I don't know," I said. "I saw a light down in the drugstore."

"Hang on," Dad said. "I'll switch to infrared, and we'll get to the bottom of this."

Dad twisted a few dials on the belt of his suit. "Wait, that's not the right one," he grumbled to himself. "That's the humidifier. Darn it, now I'm all moist. Ah, there we go—infrared."

I waited while Dad stared across the street. Finally he spoke. "What have we here? I believe we have an actual crime in progress. It looks like a couple of teens. They're in the candy aisle feeding their sweet tooth. Or would it be sweet tooths? Sweet teeth? That doesn't sound right. It doesn't matter. They haven't learned the cold, hard facts about the consequences of committing a crime when superheroes are on patrol. Come on, son. Let's go."

Before I could say anything, Dad grabbed me and stepped off the edge of the building. We flew over the top of the drugstore and landed in the alley. Sure enough, the back door was propped open with a plastic milk crate.

"You wait here," Dad said. "I'll be back in a flash."

I grabbed his sleeve. "Hey, wait! Aren't you forgetting the superhero code?"

Dad stopped up short. "What do you mean?"

"There are two superheroes on patrol," I said. "And I'm the one who spotted the crime. The superhero code says I get to make the arrest."

I could see what Dad was thinking as plain as if he'd

said it. *But you don't have a power.*

Instead, he replied, "You're right. I'll let you go in first. But I'll be right behind you if you need help. Remember your training—catch them by surprise, declare your authority, and get the situation under control."

I nodded. My hands shook, though out of fear or excitement, I wasn't sure. This could be my chance to save the day.

Opening the door, I slipped inside. Dad followed me and we found ourselves in the store's stockroom. Boxes sat on shelves, stacked almost to the ceiling. Pallets leaned against one wall. Voices drifted from the front of the store. I could just make out what the intruders were saying.

"Get a few more Hot Pockets. You know how much I love those things."

"Cheese and broccoli?"

"What are you, some kind of health nut? Get the triple meat or get nothing."

A second door led to the front of the store. I peeked through a round window that reminded me of a porthole on a boat. Two figures huddled next to a freezer unit.

The intruders were older than me—probably in high school. One of them wore a bright, puffy yellow jacket. The other had a sweater. The one with the yellow jacket poked through the freezer, while the teen wearing a sweater held a bulging pillowcase.

Yellow Jacket dumped a few packages into the

pillowcase. "Hey, you know what we forgot? Sweet Tarts!"

"Sweet Tarts?" said the teen with the sweater. "Sweet Tarts are for sissies."

"I like them," Yellow Jacket protested. "They're sweet and tart at the same time. It's a marvel of modern science."

I felt a bolt of courage. These weren't the kind of criminals who would carry weapons. These were just a couple of goofballs taking advantage of some poor shop owner. I could do this.

I looked back at Dad and gave him the thumbs-up. He returned my gesture, and nodded.

I took a deep breath. *Iron resolve. Ferocious courage. And a healthy dose of insanity.*

I adjusted my ski mask, lifted a foot, and kicked open the door. It made a satisfying crash against the wall. Both boys jumped in surprise as I stormed into the room.

"Stop right there, citizens!" My voice was strong. I felt like I had the right balance of authority and command. "We are superheroes, and you are under arrest."

Catch them by surprise, inform them of your authority, and quickly get things under control. Textbook entrance, executed to perfection.

Only it didn't work.

Sweater took one look at me and burst out laughing. "Nice ski mask, little man."

I looked behind me. Dad hadn't followed me into the room.

Yellow Jacket grinned and pointed. "I've heard of people like you. Superhero wannabes. You don't have a power, but you dress up and start pushing into other people's private affairs." He snorted. "That's a little embarrassing, kid. And your costume needs work. Are those pajamas under your pants?"

"It's thermal underwear," I said. "It keeps me toasty warm." I decided I really needed to work on my comebacks. My face felt hot under my ski mask.

For a brief moment I wondered if it had any polyester in it. Maybe I could try to impress them by striking a match on the side of my head.

"I didn't realize you freaks started so young," Yellow Jacket said. "You're an embarrassment to the real superheroes. Why don't you just go back to your mommy and—"

"Leave this kid to me."

The voice came from behind me, and it sounded mean.

I turned. What I saw made my stomach flip.

A third man with a shaved head stood leaning against a freezer. He chewed on a pencil and he had gloves with the fingers cut out. Stubble darkened his jaw.

The bald man growled. He pulled the pencil out of his mouth. "I told you guys we couldn't be seen." He took a few steps toward me. "Now things have to get a little bit messy." He returned the pencil to his mouth.

I tried backing up, but Yellow Jacket and Sweater were right there. They had me by my arms, and I couldn't break free.

The bald man was moving toward me, and then stopped short. He looked over my shoulder, and his eyes became darkened slits. I didn't need to turn around to know that Dad had finally entered the room.

"Stop right there, citizens!" Dad's voice boomed through the store. "We *are* superheroes, and you *are* under arrest."

I heard the boys gasp. They let go of me, but the bald man stepped forward. I watched as he reached behind his back and a flash of steel shined in the darkened room.

"Dad," I shouted, rolling to the side of the aisle. "He's got a gun!"

A gun. The Johnsons didn't use them, and neither did we. Dad's supersuit could stop bullets, but there were plenty of places a shot could slip through and do real damage. Dad's power was the ability to fly. Bullets would kill him just as fast as they would kill anybody else.

I couldn't look away from the barrel as the man lifted the gun and leveled it at Dad.

I'll never forget what happened next. Dad could have grabbed me and run. He could have moved to safety and called for backup. But he didn't.

Because my dad is a superhero.

He lowered his head. His helmet was titanium-and-Kevlar weave, and this would protect his face. The gun fired three times. I heard the ping of bullets hitting the metal, but in two quick steps Dad was next to the bald man. When he swung his fist, the gun went flying. Dad grabbed the man by the wrist, pulled him forward, and dropped him to the ground in a single motion.

Dad's voice was low and steady. "Nobody pulls a gun when my son's in the room. Is that understood?"

The bald man nodded.

"And take that pencil out of your mouth, you look like a beaver."

Just like that, it was over.

Dad must have already called the police, because I heard sirens in the distance. When the police arrived, Dad escorted all three of the criminals out to the patrol car. He gave one of the officers the gun.

I sat down on a crate outside and waited while Dad answered questions. The police officer wasn't very friendly, probably because now he had to fill out paper work explaining how superheroes had found and stopped a crime that he hadn't even known about. Dad answered all the questions with patience.

I closed my eyes. I could still see Dad, lowering his head, lunging forward, and saving the day. My dad was a superhero, and so was everyone else in my family. That much I knew.

Juanita had claimed her family were the superheroes. I couldn't believe it.

The Johnsons were villains, and they were up to something. Something big. If I could find out what, worthless power or not, maybe it would be my chance to save the day.

10

THIS IS BEAUTIFUL PROSE, MR. SNUGGLY BEAR

I stared at the back of Juanita's head. I'd already finished my algebra assignment, but not because Mr. Johnson was a good teacher. In fact, I was pretty sure he didn't know the first thing about algebra. All he did was read a book silently to himself and make us figure things out on our own.

I wrote a quick note.

I don't know what you're up to, but I'm going to find out.

I folded the paper and wrote *Juanita* on the outside. I tapped Hailey, the girl in front of me, on the shoulder. Mr. Johnson was still reading. I held out the note.

The man must have had eyes on the top of his head.

"Excuse me!" Mr. Johnson called from the front of the class. "You in the red shirt. What do you think you're doing?"

I pulled the note quickly back and looked down at my shirt. I already knew what color it was. Red. As red as my face. I slipped the note in my pocket.

"I asked you a question," Mr. Johnson said. "I expect an answer. What do you think you're doing?"

"Um," I said. "I just finished doing my homework for the day."

"Come up here," Mr. Johnson said. "And bring your notebook."

I stole a look at Juanita. She just shook her head as if to say, *What have you gotten yourself into?*

"Let me see your notebook," Mr. Johnson said when I got to the front of the class. I felt certain that every last student in the classroom was staring at me.

The note was still safely in my pocket, so I handed over the notebook. I spoke quietly, trying to make our conversation private. "Like I said, I already finished—"

"What have we here?" Mr. Johnson said, more to the class than to me. "Writing love notes?"

"What? No!" I protested. "That's my assignment."

Mr. Johnson held the notebook in front of him and peered over his glasses. "Dear Megan. I miss you terribly. I wish you were here by my side."

The class laughed. I glared at Juanita's uncle. I knew I'd been beat.

"I think of you all the time," Mr. Johnson continued, still pretending to read from my notebook. "I love your beautiful ears, your pointy little nose, and your ankles. I could stare at your ankles all day."

The class was laughing hard now. Mike sat in the front row. He wasn't laughing, but he wouldn't look at me. None of my classmates would stand with me. I didn't care. I was a superhero. Sometimes a superhero had to stand alone.

Mr. Johnson wasn't done. "I wish I could hold you in my arms while I do my algebra assignment. I don't really understand these problems, and you're so smart. I miss, miss, miss you. Yours truly, Mr. Snuggly Bear."

The class roared with laughter—the kind of laughter kids do when they're glad it's somebody else who's being made fun of and not them.

"This is beautiful prose, Mr. Snuggly Bear," Mr. Johnson said. "But may I remind you this is algebra and not Creative Writing? Please return to your seat and do your assignment."

Mr. Johnson tore my assignment out of the notebook, crumpled it up, and tossed it in the trash.

I felt a twinge of anger. "You can't just—"

"Oh, but I can," Mr. Johnson said. His lips turned into a cruel smile. "And if Mr. Snuggly Bear doesn't return to his seat, I'll send him to the principal's office." He handed the empty notebook to me.

"Un—I mean, Mr. Johnson." Juanita stood at her desk. "You can't do this. It's not *right*."

Mr. Johnson frowned. "Thank you for your opinion, Juanita, but you know what kind of . . . person this is."

Juanita held her ground. "It doesn't matter who he is, this isn't right."

The class was silent. I could see confusion in their faces. There was probably confusion in my face too.

Mr. Johnson stared at Juanita. He finally picked up his book and sat back in his chair. "Mr. Snuggly Bear, if you wish to retrieve your love letter from the trash, you are free to do so. But I don't want any more trouble from you, is that understood?"

I fished my assignment from the trash and returned to my seat. Juanita sat at her desk. She didn't turn around.

I flattened my assignment out on my desk, and then pulled the note to Juanita from my pocket and read it again.

The note was even truer now than when I'd written it just a few minutes ago. I had *no* idea what Juanita was up to. I tore up the first note, wrote my phone number on a piece of paper, and slipped it into my pocket.

I stared at the back of Juanita's head and worked out my next move.

11

EYES ON THE JOHNSONS, NOT THE PAPER TOWELS

Turns out I didn't have to make the next move. Dad made it for me. It was a bold and decisive move. It was the move that changed everything.

That afternoon, he took me and Benny grocery shopping.

Shopping is a pretty easy chore since my family only eats about nine different things—like potatoes, chard, jicama, brown rice, and goat's milk. We'd already loaded the cart with asparagus and evaporated milk, and Dad was loading six jars of green olives into the cart when he froze. He looked over my shoulder, toward the freezer section. I turned around and saw Juanita Johnson and her father.

When a supervillain stares down a superhero, you might

expect there to be a lot of fighting or shouting right from the beginning. But that's not how it goes, at least not when the supers aren't in costume. They can't trade insults, because that would give away their secret identities.

Dad stared at Juanita's father, and Juanita's father stared back at Dad. The silence became uncomfortable.

Dad finally spoke, his voice cold. "Hello, Caesar."

"Hello, William," the Johnson replied, matching Dad's tone.

I'd never met Juanita's father, but Dad was apparently on a first-name basis with him.

While the two adults traded glares, I looked at Juanita. She rolled her eyes.

Dad spoke quietly, so only Benny and I could hear. "Let's walk away slowly, boys, but don't break eye contact. You never break eye contact with a villain—it's a sign of weakness."

"I think that's for when you're dealing with wild animals," I said, but Dad ignored me.

He pushed the cart carefully, twisting around so he could watch Juanita and her father. One of the wheels on Dad's cart made a squeaking sound with every rotation.

"Uh, Dad?" Benny said. "You're headed straight for the paper-towel display."

"Eyes on the Johnsons," Dad said. "Not the paper towels."

True to his own advice, Dad never took his eyes off the Johnsons. His cart hit the tall tower of paper towels, which fell to the floor with a fluffy crash. He scrambled to build the paper towels back into a tower, but he kept one eye on the Johnsons, who were walking in the other direction, and the tower kept falling over.

The Johnsons disappeared around the corner and Dad gave up on the tower. He kicked the pile and the paper towels went flying in all directions. Dad bent over and looked at Benny and me. "The Johnsons are up to no good. We've got to figure out what they're planning."

Dad left our cart and walked quickly down the pet-food aisle. Benny followed. I brought up the rear. When we got to the back of the store, the Johnsons were gone.

"This isn't good," Dad said. "Benny, call Grandpa and tell him what's going on. I've got to go change."

Benny pulled out his phone and tapped the screen. "Where are you going?" Benny asked me.

"I need to talk to Juanita."

"You can't talk to her," Benny whispered. "If Dad catches you, you'll be grounded for a year."

"Stay here," I told Benny. "Keep an eye out for Dad."

I walked slowly down the back of the store, looking down each aisle.

I found her standing by the cold cereal. Our eyes met. She looked behind her, and then back to me. She hadn't tried to run, and she didn't look afraid. But she also didn't make a move to communicate.

Iron resolve, ferocious courage, and a healthy dose of insanity.

Benny and I used to stay up late at night when we were younger, coming up with insults we would hurl at the Johnsons during the heat of battle. But here I was about to have a civilized conversation with a supervillain. I walked toward Juanita.

"Hello," I said.

"Hello," Juanita replied. I'm usually pretty good at reading people, but her face told me nothing.

"You never told us what your power was yesterday."

Juanita shrugged. "Maybe I didn't want to."

"We told you ours. It's only fair that—"

"Nothing's fair when you're dealing with supervillains," Juanita said.

"Ha!" I said, then lowered my voice. We were alone in the aisle, but I didn't want anybody overhearing. "So you admit it, you're a supervillain?"

Juanita shook her head. "No, *I* don't have to play fair, because *you* are the supervillain. If you're dumb enough to tell me your power, it doesn't mean I have to turn around and tell you mine."

My face grew warm. "So you're still going to try to tell me that my family are the supervillains?"

"Look, it's not that hard," Juanita said. "We both have worthless powers. You leave me alone, I'll leave you alone."

The tactics side of my brain flickered. Juanita had discovered that Benny and I had worthless powers. Now she wanted us to leave her alone so that she could . . . so that she could do what?

"Benny and I are sworn protectors of the city." It sounded a little corny when I said it, but I kept talking. "We're not going to just sit back and let you carry out some crazy scheme."

Juanita rolled her eyes, then pointed. "I think your brother wants to talk to you."

I turned around. Benny motioned for me to come to him. He looked desperate. There were a million questions I wanted to ask Juanita.

I put my hand in my pocket and pulled out the slip of paper with my phone number. I handed it to Juanita. She took it, but her face was like stone. I walked toward Benny. He grabbed me by the arm and pulled me around the corner. "Juanita's dad is heading this way," he said.

I peeked back into the aisle. Juanita was gone. Benny and I walked across the front of the store and spotted Mr. Johnson, dressed in his supersuit, scanning the produce section.

"Citizen!" Caesar's voice exploded through the store as he pointed at one of the shoppers. Everybody picking through fruits and vegetables stopped and looked at the supervillain. "What have you got in your hands?"

The shopper stared at Juanita's dad, his mouth hanging open. He held a kiwi in one hand, and a plastic bag in the other.

Caesar strode toward the man, who looked quite nervous. "Up to no good, are we?"

"Uh . . ." said the man. "No, sir. I'm just buying some fruit—a kiwi." He held up the furry brown fruit in an effort to prove his point.

"You look a little shady to me," Caesar said.

"I'm not shady," said the man. He looked hurt. "I promise. I'm very . . . *unshady*."

Caesar walked around the man, looking him up and down. "Look at those clothes—a bit on the dingy side, aren't they? And that beard? Very scruffy. And what about that hat? That's a shifty hat if I ever saw one."

"My mother knitted me this hat," the man said. "For my birthday."

Juanita's dad leaned over and squinted at the hat. "Your mother is a shifty knitter."

A second booming, authoritative voice boomed. "What have we here?"

Dad entered the produce section. Standing in his supersuit, he looked heroic as always. I had a funny mental image of Dad and Mr. Johnson changing into their supersuits in neighboring bathroom stalls.

"Shoppers," Dad said, "I suggest you leave quickly before this villain does you harm. There's no need to panic . . . well, maybe a little need to panic."

That was all the shoppers needed. They left carts behind and headed for the door. The man with the kiwi looked especially glad that Dad had shown up.

"Come on, Benny," I said, tugging at my brother's shirt. "Let's go wait in the car."

"But Dad might need our help," Benny said.

"We don't have any powers," I reminded Benny, although I suspected that wouldn't stop Benny from trying. "Besides, we also don't have our supersuits. We'd blow our cover."

Benny scowled, but followed me as I turned to leave.

I heard Dad and Caesar begin the verbal sparring behind me.

"Watch it, buster," Dad said, "or I'll be forced to engage you in a physical confrontation."

"Confront away. You are no match for my thunderquick reflexes."

"Do you mean lightning-quick? You need to work on your metaphors, villain."

"I mean exactly what I say. My reflexes are better than lightning. Lightning is just a flash of light. My reflexes are more like a crushing wave of thunder!"

"So your reflexes kick in five to ten seconds after they

are actually needed? Now that you mention it, you do have thunder-quick reflexes."

"Hey now—"

"Grandpa is sending a team," Benny said when we got to the door. "They should be here soon."

We left the store and climbed into our car. A few minutes later, a stream of water poured out the front doors.

"I think Juanita's dad has the ability to make it rain," I said.

"Even all those paper towels aren't going to be able to clean up this mess," Benny said.

People drove their cars out of the parking lot. I noticed a Volkswagen beetle pulling *in* to the parking lot. The car was green and rusted, and the license plate read U8A BUG.

Three Johnsons—it looked like a mom, a dad, and their teenage son—stepped out of the car. They were dressed in supersuits.

"Uh-oh," Benny said. "That makes it Dad against an entire team of Johnsons."

The three Johnsons entered the store. I'd seen Dad in battle dozens of times, and he'd never gotten hurt. Still, I felt a pinch of fear.

The automatic doors to the store opened. For a moment nothing happened, but then a six-foot ball of ice came flying through the opening, slamming against the Volkswagen. I saw movement in the back of the car.

Juanita was in there, shaking her head as if a gigantic ice ball was a mere annoyance.

Four Johnsons came strutting out of the store like cowboys from an old western saloon.

"Is that Dad in the ice?" Benny asked.

I could see our family colors reflecting from inside the frozen water. "Looks like it," I said.

Juanita got out of her car and moved farther away from the store. I didn't have time to think. I opened the back door of our car. "Juanita," I called. "Over here."

"What are you doing?" Benny whispered.

"Trying to find out the truth," I said.

Juanita looked over her shoulder, and then ran to our car, got in, and closed the door.

The block of ice that was Dad slowly flew into the air. He went up about ten feet, and then came crashing back to the asphalt parking lot. The ice shattered and Dad came rolling out on top. He stood up and put his hands on his hips. "Everybody's always telling me how cool I am."

I groaned and Juanita stifled a laugh. I was starting to wonder if I'd inherited poor comebacks from Dad.

The teenage Johnson flipped his wrist and thin ropes came shooting out of his palm. He cracked the ropes like whips and stepped forward. He slung one of the ropes and it wrapped around Dad's legs.

"Gotcha," the boy said.

"Yes." Dad grinned. "Yes you do. Now let's see if you can keep me."

With that he sprang into the air, hauling the Johnson behind him.

The Johnson teen screamed loud and long all the way up.

Juanita watched the action out the window but didn't seem all that interested.

"What were you doing at the store today?" I asked. I doubted she'd tell me, but maybe I could trap her in a lie.

Juanita looked at me. "The same thing you were doing," she said. "Shopping."

"For what?" I asked.

"Umm . . . for groceries? It's a grocery store. Do you want me to go get our list?"

It was harder to trap somebody in a lie than I thought.

"What about you?" she asked. "If anybody was acting suspicious, it was you Baileys." She cracked open her door, spit, and closed it again. "Nobody buys that much evaporated milk and asparagus."

"It's part of the superhero diet," Benny explained. "Mom makes this really good asparagus casserole. Sometimes she puts cornflakes on top and—"

"And the point is," I interrupted, "we were doing the same thing. Grocery shopping."

Benny pointed out the window. "Here comes the cavalry," he said.

A minivan came skidding to a halt in front of the store. Uncle Ralph and Aunt Carole climbed out, followed closely by Jessie.

"What have we herrrrrrrrre!" The voice came from next to the minivan.

"Who said that?" Juanita asked.

"That's my aunt Verna," Benny said. "She's invisible."

I watched out the front windshield as the three Johnsons standing by the store each jumped as if somebody had whacked them on the back of the head. Then they ran inside.

The battle was in full swing now. Dad flew around with the poor Johnson hanging on with his ropes. Dad flew close to trees, dragging the Johnson through the branches and limbs. The Johnson kept yelling, "Put me down!" But Dad looked like he was having too much fun.

Someone had propped the store doors open. Snow and ice were flying out of the store while Jessie's lightning kept flying in.

"Have you guys ever wondered about all of this?" Juanita asked.

"All of what?" I asked.

Juanita waved her hand. "All of this. The fighting. You guys never win. We never win. Sure, we drive you away sometimes, or you drive us away. But we just keep fighting and fighting."

"Superhero code," Benny said, matter-of-factly. "We respect all life, even a supervillain's."

Juanita nodded. "Yeah, so do we. I guess that would explain why nobody ever gets hurt."

I felt like I was missing something—that something wasn't right. "There's no way that our families could be fighting for decades and decades and not realize that the other family thinks they're superheroes too."

To my surprise, Juanita nodded. "I've been thinking the same thing. It doesn't make sense."

She looked out the window again. Behind her I saw Dad swoop low and drop the hanging Johnson in the top of a tree. It would take him a few minutes to climb down. The Johnson yelled and spit as Dad flew back into the sky.

Juanita looked bored, like there wasn't a superhero battle raging just a dozen feet away.

"It looks like your family has won this round," she said.

As the three Johnsons piled back into the Volkswagen, Jessie kept blasting lightning at their feet, and they hopped around trying to keep their knees and legs high in the air.

Juanita's dad raced for his car. He tripped once, probably thanks to Aunt Verna, and then scrambled for his keys.

"I have to go," Juanita said.

"Wait," I said. "What is your power? At least tell us that."

Juanita looked back at me, and then got out of the car. She raced to her vehicle and slipped inside. In another moment, the Johnsons had left, and Dad was shaking hands with Uncle Ralph and patting Jessie on the back.

"Do you trust her?" Benny asked.

I didn't know what to think. "I think she's up to something."

My phone buzzed. I pulled it out of my pocket. I had a text message from an unlisted number. I pressed the button to read the screen.

You want to see my power? Get on the 1080 bus tomorrow after school.

12

ONE OF US IS ABOUT TO
BE DISAPPOINTED

The 1080 went downtown. It also stopped at the public library, so Benny and I weren't totally lying when we asked our parents if we could head there after school. We just didn't mention the very small fact that we would be riding with a Johnson. That's a conversation I'd rather not have.

The public bus smelled like every other bus I'd ever been on—stale air that carried the scent of humans in coats, newspapers, and also the slightest hint of adventure.

Juanita sat alone at the back of the bus, her dark curls poking just above the seats. It was a perfect place for an ambush, but I didn't see any other suspicious-looking people. I checked the bus driver twice. The last thing I wanted was to be trapped in a bus driven by a Johnson.

Benny and I took a seat across the aisle from Juanita. No one else was within hearing distance.

Without breaking eye contact, I took in everything I could. Juanita had on a black woolen coat, pink gloves, and a backpack. The backpack looked like it held nothing more than books, but I couldn't be sure.

"Hello," Juanita said.

"Hello," I replied, realizing this is exactly how our conversation had started in the grocery store. Then again . . . a lot of conversations start that way. "You wanted to meet us here?" I couldn't read her face.

"You wanted to see my power," she said.

I nodded. "Do you have to show it to us on a bus?" That sounded silly, but if she'd gotten powers that were as silly as ours, then anything was possible.

Juanita shook her head. "I can't just show it to you," Juanita said. "It wouldn't prove anything."

"Why not?" I asked.

"Because." She lowered her voice. "If I'm really a Super-super, I can do any power. So I'd show you a single worthless power, but you would still wonder if I could do all the other powers."

I hadn't thought of that. I looked over at Benny, who just shrugged.

"Then where are we going?" I asked. "How are you

going to prove you've only got one power?"

"I'll tell you when we get there," Juanita said. "It's not far."

Benny leaned forward in his seat and held up his pointer finger. "Just for the record," he said, "we're not afraid of you."

I thought I saw a hint of a smile on Juanita's lips. "I'm glad to hear that, Benny," she said. "You shouldn't be."

That sounded to me like something a spider would tell a fly—right before the fly became dinner.

An elderly gentleman came and sat near the back and we couldn't talk about powers anymore. We rode in silence.

Four stops later, Juanita stood. "This is it," she said.

Benny and I followed Juanita off the bus. We were in a nice part of the city, just north of downtown. Fences of stone or iron surrounded the homes. Juanita came to a stop in front of a large gate. The property was well maintained. I could just make out a towering, sleek-looking house, sitting back among some trees.

"This is my grandmother's house," Juanita said. "It's our headquarters."

Benny's eyes grew wide, and I couldn't stop from laughing. "Oh, so you just brought us right to your headquarters? We've been looking for this place for years. You wouldn't just . . ."

Juanita wasn't even listening to me. She pressed her

palm to a glowing pad built into the side of a stone wall. The iron gate opened and she walked through.

Benny stepped forward but I grabbed the sleeve of his coat. "Benny," I whispered. "What if we're walking into a trap?"

Benny shrugged. "We're superheroes. Walking into traps is in our job description."

"You're crazy," I said. "You know that, right?"

I felt for the phone in my pocket. The weight gave me courage. We could always call for help.

Looking around one last time, I followed Benny through the gate.

Juanita led us across a cobbled walkway toward the front door.

"This looks like a mansion," Benny said. The house was made of gray stone with wooden shingles. It had two stories with massive chimneys sticking out of the roof every twenty feet.

Juanita spoke over her shoulder. "When I was little, I used to think this was a castle, and my grandmother was a queen."

"And what's your grandmother going to say when we walk in your front door?" I asked.

"Hopefully nobody is going to see you," Juanita said. "But if you'd rather wait out here, that's fine with me. Just don't try to leave—the alarm will sound. And then they'll probably let the dogs loose, and that won't be fun for you at all."

"How are we supposed to move around your headquarters without being seen?" Benny asked.

Juanita shrugged. "We'll wing it."

We'll wing it.

"Why does everybody keep saying that?" I mumbled.

For what felt like the hundredth time, Juanita ignored me. She pushed open the door and went inside. Benny followed. Casting one last look over my shoulder, I entered too.

I heard Benny gasp. As soon as my eyes adjusted, I saw why.

Covering every square inch of the entryway were hundreds of portraits in various shapes and sizes. Some had large frames with delicate carvings. Others were framed by polished black wood or even simple brown.

"There must be a thousand," Benny said.

"Not a thousand," Juanita said. "Although I've never been able to count them all. I always get mixed up around two hundred."

The faces made me nervous. It felt like hundreds of eyes followed me wherever I went. And not just hundreds of eyes . . . hundreds of Johnson eyes.

I stepped closer and examined a few of the paintings. One picture had a man with a round face and a toothy grin. I thought he looked familiar. His face was jolly, but each of his pupils had a hint of red. Another painting had a woman dressed in a brown velvet dress. Everything in the picture was crisp and sharp, but the woman herself was blurry. I looked closer but it didn't help.

The largest portrait hung in the middle of the wall; a soft white light shone down on it from the ceiling. An old woman holding a glass cane sat on what looked like a throne. Behind her were towering clouds rising from a green field.

If this was Juanita's grandmother, I could understand why Juanita thought she was a queen.

"Who are all of these people?" I asked.

"My relatives," Juanita said. "Some live here in Split Rock, but most are in other parts of the state or even farther. The portraits look normal enough that we can have them hanging out here in the open, but if you look closely, you can see the power of each person hidden in the portrait."

The man with red pupils. I'd seen him before when watching battle footage. He could shoot lasers out of his eyes. And the woman who was blurry—probably a Speedy.

"Is this your grandmother?" I asked, pointing to the largest painting.

Juanita nodded. "She can control the weather."

"Hey," Benny said. "Is that why it's always raining at our family reunions?"

Juanita smiled. "Grandmother has better things to do than make it rain at your reunions."

Benny touched my arm and pointed to a polished metal vase sitting against the wall. As soon as I saw it, I realized there were more of them spread throughout the room. They were silver in color and about six inches tall.

Benny raised his eyebrows and I shrugged my shoulders.

"So can we see your power?" I asked. "Benny and I can't be gone long."

"I want to show you two things," Juanita said. "My cousin Victor finished my painting two days ago. It shows what my power is, and it's downstairs."

I didn't bother mentioning that her cousin Victor could have painted anything. "What's the second thing?"

"I'll tell you after the painting," Juanita said. She led the way to an elevator and pushed the down button, opening the doors. We stepped inside and the doors closed behind us. Earlier I'd felt trapped. Now I felt downright claustrophobic.

I noticed another silver vase in the elevator.

Juanita turned to a small panel of buttons. She pressed the fire-alarm button, the close-door button, the second-floor button twice, and then the fire alarm again. A secret panel slid open next to Juanita, revealing more buttons than I'd ever seen in an elevator.

"Whoa!" Benny said, pointing at the large bank of buttons. The very last one had 104 printed on it. "I thought there were only two floors."

"My uncle Jared explains it the best," Juanita said. "Our headquarters is like a skyscraper, but only the top two floors are above ground."

"Can I push the button?" Benny asked. "Dad never lets me push the button."

"We're going to level twenty-eight," Juanita said. "No wait, level twenty-nine."

Benny had already pushed the twenty-eight button. He pressed twenty-nine as well. "What's on level twenty-eight?"

The elevator shuddered as we descended deep into the Johnson headquarters. For the first time on this trip, Juanita looked nervous. "Actually, I can't remember. I always get lost in this place. But maybe you'd better hide, just in case."

"We're in an elevator," I said. "Where exactly are we supposed to hide?"

Juanita looked at the panel. "I don't know, but you have about six more seconds."

The elevator dinged. There was no time to think. Benny and I split up on either side of the door, our backs pressed against the wall. I looked at the back of the elevator, which was polished metal. In the reflection, I could just make out what was happening on level twenty-eight.

Four people sat at a table. One of them shot bubbles into the air from a plastic bubble launcher. A small robot that looked like a dog jumped up and down on the table, snatching at each bubble with razor-sharp teeth. The other people at the table cheered the robot on.

At the sound of the door opening, they all turned and looked at the elevator. No one seemed to notice our reflections.

Juanita waved. "Sorry about that. Wrong level."

"No worries," one of them said, and the doors closed.

"That's right," Juanita said. "Level twenty-eight is research and development. That's a weird place to hang out."

I felt a twinge of jealousy. We didn't have anything nearly as cool as a robotic dog. I'd always been proud of my family because we kept the Johnsons from destroying the city. But now . . . now it felt like maybe my family wasn't as amazing as I'd first thought.

The doors opened again on level twenty-nine, and Juanita stepped out of the elevator. She looked around and then motioned for Benny and me to follow.

This room had high ceilings, making it feel like we were inside a warehouse. Pieces of canvas and half-finished portraits rested against large crates scattered around the floor. A table covered with tubes of paint stood against one wall. In the very middle of the room was a painting with a cloth draped over the top of it.

I counted four more silver vases on the floor.

Footsteps came from farther back in the studio. Juanita

took a sharp breath. "Hide!" She whispered. "Quick!"

I lunged for one of the crates. There was enough space between the wall and the box for me to crouch without being seen. I peeked around the corner and looked for Benny.

My brother's head poked out from behind a large canvas leaning against the far wall. He waved and gave me the thumbs-up. I put my fingers to my lips. He nodded and hunkered down.

A woman stepped into view. I recognized her from the portrait downstairs—Juanita's grandmother. She didn't wear a crown, but she still looked like a queen. She wore a deep-blue dress, and her black and gray hair was wrapped in a tight bun. Standing straight and tall, she held a glass walking cane as if it were a scepter.

From my place behind the crate I could see both Juanita and her grandmother, but it was dark enough that I didn't think her grandmother would see me. Benny was completely blocked from their view.

"Ah, Juanita," Grandmother Johnson said. "I see you got Victor's message. I'm so glad you came, sweetheart."

I know it sounds strange, but the most surprising thing was hearing Grandma Johnson, queen of the supervillains, call her granddaughter *sweetheart*. I'd always pictured the leader of the Split Rock Johnsons as a witch.

"I'd like to be alone, Grandmother." Juanita said. If she was nervous about sneaking two Baileys into the Johnson headquarters, she didn't show it.

"And I'd like some company," Grandma Johnson said. "One of us is about to be disappointed, and I'll let you in on a little secret. . . . It isn't going to be me."

Here I was staring at the leader of the Johnson clan—the woman who'd led the fight against my family for who knows how many years—and I couldn't help but like her.

"It's time to talk about this, honey." Grandmother Johnson tapped her cane on the floor. "You seem awfully disappointed for a girl who didn't even want a power in the first place."

I looked over at Benny. He stared back at me, a look of confusion covering his face. Every kid in the city wanted to be super. What was Juanita's grandmother talking about?

"I told you last week that no matter what power you got, you would be able to help this family," Grandmother Johnson said. "I still believe that."

"This power was a sign," Juanita said. "I don't want to be super, and this power just shows that the universe doesn't want me to be either."

"It doesn't matter what we want," Grandmother Johnson said. "We are the only ones who can stand up to those Baileys."

She reared her head back, threw it forward, and spit. I heard a small *ting*.

The silver vases. They weren't vases at all. They were spittoons.

Juanita started pacing the room, her hands clasped behind her, her face scrunched, like Benny when he was working on math.

"You have two villains at your school," Grandmother Johnson continued. I squirmed at the idea of being called a villain. "You have received your power, and now you need to stand up and join us in our fight. Whether you think you can or not."

"It's not a question of whether I think I can, Grandmother," Juanita said, and I heard anger rising in her voice. "I don't want anything to do with this."

I wondered if Juanita had forgotten that Benny and I were still in the room.

"You are a Johnson, my child," Juanita's grandmother said. "You are super. You don't have a choice in the matter."

"I do have a choice in the matter, and I won't do it." Juanita continued her pacing, walking in a tight figure eight around her grandmother and then around the concealed portrait. "No matter how hard we fight, it's never good enough. We've been fighting for decades."

"Then we keep fighting," Grandmother Johnson said. "We are up to the challenge."

"No matter how good we are, sometimes people still get hurt." Juanita's voice broke, and now I knew she'd forgotten Benny and I were in the room. She was on the verge of tears. "No matter how super we are, sometimes people still die."

Juanita stopped. Her head pointed to the floor. Her hair covered her face, but I could hear harsh breathing. Juanita wiped at her eyes.

Grandmother Johnson broke the silence. "You know there was nothing any of us could do to save your mother."

I held my breath.

"I know." Juanita's voice was almost a whisper. "But if she hadn't tried to save that driver . . . If she'd just stayed home instead of trying to be super . . ."

"Your mother wasn't *trying* to be super," Grandmother Johnson said. "She *was* super. Your mother saw that accident and saved three people before the explosion. She . . ." Grandmother Johnson stopped, then cleared her throat. "Your mother used her powers for good. Always for good. Just as you must use your power to—"

Juanita almost flew to the cloth-covered portrait. "To what?" Juanita was shouting now. "What am I supposed to do with *this*?"

With a single tug she ripped off the cloth from the easel, revealing the painting beneath.

I couldn't tear my gaze away from the portrait.

Her cousin Victor had placed the painting right under a soft white light, and it seemed to glow in the middle of the room.

In the painting Juanita stood in a field of flowers. She wore a pink dress, and her hair was curled and fell down past her shoulders. At school, every time Juanita looked at me she was either scowling or spitting. But Victor had captured a beautiful smile and shining face. In the background, jets of water shot up from behind her, forming a magnificent arc. From where I was hiding the droplets of water seemed so real it looked like somebody had sprayed water on the canvas.

"Do you know what Victor's power is?" Grandmother put her hand on Juanita's shoulder. Juanita stared at the painting and held the palms of her hands to her cheeks. She didn't answer for several moments.

"Painting is his power," Juanita said. "No one can paint like Victor."

"That's what most of the relatives think," Grandmother Johnson said. "Victor is a private person, and he doesn't bother to correct them. But that's not the case. He's spent years working on his art. I have some of his early work that looks like it was painted by an elephant with a stiff trunk. No, his real power lies in the ability to see what others cannot. With a simple glance, he sees into the heart and soul of another person.

"Cousin Victor looked into your heart," Grandmother Johnson said. "And this is what he painted. Now look at that portrait and tell me the little girl in there doesn't have something important to offer the world."

Juanita said nothing.

"You have a lot to think about," Grandmother Johnson said. "I'm going to leave you alone. When you're ready to talk again, you let me know."

The elevator dinged, and Grandmother Johnson was gone. Juanita stood in front of the painting. She stared at the portrait, but I don't think she saw it.

I crawled out from my hiding place and went to stand next to her.

"It's a very nice painting," I said, and Juanita jumped.

Benny came forward until his nose almost touched the portrait.

"What is your power?" Benny said. "Are you a Gusher? Because if you are, that's just plain cool."

Juanita shook her head. She continued to stare at the painting, but I don't think she really saw it.

"We don't have a name for my power," Juanita said. "I guess if we did, it would be a Flusher."

"A what?" Benny and I said at the same time.

I looked closely at the painting. At the base of each stream of water wasn't a small fountainhead like I first thought. They were toilets. Tiny little toilets.

I saw sadness in Juanita's face.

"If a toilet is backed up, and I pull the handle, the pipes become clear," Juanita said. "I'm a super Flusher."

13

IT'S BEEN A ROUGH WEEK

I was missing something. I almost wanted to believe Juanita—even though her claim was outrageous—but I was missing something. I could feel it.

Juanita walked over and pressed the elevator button. The door opened, and we walked inside. Juanita pushed floor seventy-two.

"Where are we going now?" Benny asked.

"I'm going to show you the second thing," Juanita said. "I'm going to prove to you that I'm telling the truth, and then I want to be left alone."

I looked at Juanita in the reflection of the elevator doors. She looked at the floor. I thought about what she'd said about her mother. I wanted to ask her about the accident. But part of me wanted to pretend that superheroes never got hurt.

In the end, I decided if Juanita ever wanted to tell me, I'd listen.

The doors opened, and Juanita led us down a long, narrow corridor, pausing a couple times as if she heard a sound. There were doors on either side of the hall, and Juanita opened the third one on the left and ushered us into a room that looked like the computer lab at school.

"What is this?" I asked.

"What does it look like?" Juanita said, then she looked over at me. Our eyes met, and I think for the first time, I saw the real Juanita. A tired girl, who had feelings and fears and was in over her head. "I'm sorry," she said. "It's been a rough week."

"I understand," I said. "Us too."

Juanita sat down at a computer and opened several browser windows. She entered some user names and passwords, logging into several different systems, and then stood up.

"There you go," Juanita said. "I've given you access to our entire system. You have emails, calendar items, files . . . everything."

I didn't quite know what to do. Benny coughed behind me. It didn't feel right to just start snooping around in their personal files.

"I'm not going to let you just do anything," Juanita said. "But if you look through all our files, you'll see we have no plans for doing anything wrong. You'll see that all our communication is about how to stop the villains—you guys. There's over five hundred gigabytes of information. You know we couldn't fake that."

I sat at the computer and started clicking. Benny eventually sat down at another computer and opened an online game.

At first I looked through the files. As far as I could tell, there weren't any blueprints for death rays, or plans for world domination. There was quite a collection of music, and I noticed that the Johnson family seemed to like the classics—Mozart, Tchaikovsky, Vivaldi. There were also a lot of pictures—birthdays, family reunions. I found a map of the city where they'd made guesses about our headquarters' location. I was pleased to see they weren't even close.

I opened the browser where Juanita had logged into the email system.

"I don't want to go reading through people's personal emails," I said. "That doesn't feel right."

I thought I saw the hint of a smile on Juanita's face. "I'm glad to hear that," Juanita said. "Here . . ."

Juanita took the keyboard and typed in a few commands. "This is the email account we use for all our official superhero communication—to the mayor, the city council, that sort of thing. There's nothing personal."

The emails proved much more interesting. I got lost in scrolling through them. There were messages to the mayor asking for support in "fighting the villains." There were proposals to the chief of police, the governor, and anybody else who would listen, proposing ways to capture and imprison the "supervillains" once and for all.

But that wasn't the most interesting part.

"What is an *armistice*?" Benny asked, reading over my shoulder. "Is that one of those things you attach to your arm so that you can hit harder?"

Juanita shook her head. "Armistice—that means to stop fighting."

I pointed to the screen. "I'm seeing five emails by a guy named Oscar Redding. Last summer he wrote to your family several times asking for an armistice. He wanted both families to sit down and talk. Your family said they wouldn't agree to anything until our family agreed. I wonder if he ever wrote to us."

"The name sounds familiar," Juanita said. She took the keyboard from me again. With a few quick keystrokes, she had a new window up. "Looks like he's in the chamber of commerce. He owns several businesses in town. Ah, he also owns the thermal underwear factory. Or rather owned it. We destroyed it last year, remember?"

"Yeah," I said.

"That makes sense," Benny said. "We destroyed his factory, so he wanted us to stop fighting."

My phone buzzed. I read the screen.

Dinner in an hour. Don't be late, your father has a surprise. —Mom

I didn't want a surprise. I wanted answers.

14

THAT'S NOT A SURPRISE, THAT'S A KICK IN THE TEETH

Juanita led us back to the street, and Benny and I rode the bus home in silence. I felt like I had all the pieces to a puzzle, but I couldn't get them to fit. By the time I got off the bus, I was as confused as ever.

That night at dinner, Dad hinted twice at the surprise.

"Our supersuits?" Benny's eyes were hungry. "Are our supersuits down in the root cellar?"

"Ah, ah, ah," said Dad, making a mock scolding motion with his finger. "No questions until after dinner."

Benny ate with gusto, shoveling food into his mouth like it was a race. After dinner, Rodney stayed upstairs to clear the table and do the dishes. Dad and Mom led

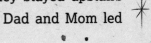

Benny and me down to the main room of the root cellar. Dad leaned against a worktable and tried a little too hard to look casual. Mom sat in a chair and smiled, but she looked nervous. Like she was about to put on a big show.

Clearing his throat, Dad said, "As you boys know, this family has a wide variety of superpowers. And those superpowers are used for different purposes."

Benny raised his hand, but Dad ignored him. I could tell he'd planned out this speech and would keep on talking until he was finished. "Many of the family's super-powers are quite useful during battles, but other powers work better in the special-ops missions—like Great-uncle Pete over in Oak City. He can shrink to roughly the size of a taco. When we need somebody to sneak into small places, he's our man."

Dad clasped his hands behind his back. "Other pow-ers—like your brother Rodney's, for example—are much better suited for background work. Rodney is an impor-tant member of our team, even though he almost never gets to go to the battles."

"But he still gets to go every once in a while," Benny said, choosing his words carefully. "And he still has a supersuit."

Dad looked at Mom as if asking for help. Mom said nothing. Finally Dad looked back to Benny. "Your mother and I have had a long talk, and we've discussed it with a few other members of the family. I think for right now it's better to have you boys stay away from the battles—where it's safe."

Benny smiled and nodded. I think I was as surprised as Dad and Mom. Then I saw Benny's eyes grow wide.

"Wait," he cried. "You mean we never get to go to a battle?"

"Well," Dad said. "I don't know if you'll *never* get to go to a battle, but for now, it's just not—"

Benny was out of his chair in a flash. "That's not fair!" Desperate, he looked in my direction. "Rafter, tell them. The battles aren't even dangerous. The Johnsons aren't trying to kill us. They think they're superheroes too."

Now wasn't the best time to try to explain anything to my parents, but I couldn't leave my brother out to dry.

"He's right," I said. "Dad, you told me on patrol that I should find out for myself. I don't know all the answers yet, but something isn't right. I think we should try to sit down and talk with the Johnsons."

Dad rubbed the sides of his head with the tips of his fingers. "Dear, can you help me out here?"

Mom finally spoke. "The other thing to remember, Benny dear, is that you're both due for a growth spurt. We wouldn't want to get you a supersuit and then have you grow right out of it."

"Growth spurt?" Benny said, almost shouting. "I

don't get a supersuit because I'm due for a growth spurt?"

"We've come up with another way you can help this family," Dad said. "And this is the big surprise."

Benny folded his arms tightly across his chest and glared at Dad. I hoped for Benny's sake that Dad had come up with a suitable replacement for not getting suits.

"When we go on the special-ops missions," Dad said, "we usually drive in a big van. There's plenty of room in there, and the team usually does some last-minute prep work on the ride to the location—you know, check their gear, do a few stretching exercises, things like that."

"You don't want to pull a hamstring in the middle of a special-ops mission," Mom said, nodding at Benny and me.

Dad continued. "But whoever is driving can't prep. Sometimes they show up, and the whole team has to wait while they double-check their gear. So your mother and I have decided that you boys can become experts at all the motor-pool vehicles. When you're old enough to drive, you can prove yourselves very valuable by . . ."

"*That's* the surprise?" Benny asked, his eyes bugging out. "We get to work in the motor pool?"

"The motor pool is a very fun place," Mom said.

Benny's mouth hung open. "That's not a surprise, that's a kick in the teeth. I can't even drive for four more years!"

"In the meantime," Dad said, "You'll start by learning the different machines, keeping them maintained and clean, checking the oil and tire pressure, things like that."

For the past three years I'd had a mental image of what I'd look like as a superhero. I'd imagined what my supersuit would look like. I'd imagined the heroic things I'd do. And now that mental image was replaced with a new image. I could see it as clear as the cowlick on the top of Dad's head—me in overalls, grease covering my hands and face. I had a wrench in my hand, and I was working on Uncle Chambers's Datsun.

Our family had really boring cars. We had to so that we could fit in. And now I got to work on these really boring cars.

Rafter Bailey—mechanic to the superheroes.

"So we're supposed to wash cars and change oil until we're old enough to drive?" Benny said. "And then we'll drive everybody to the really cool missions and just wait in the car?" I could tell Benny was close to crying. "Maybe when we finally do get our supersuits—after our growth spurts—they will come with cute little chauffeur hats."

Dad's voice became firm. "Your cousin Dirk is in charge of the family motor pool up at Grandpa's ranch. Starting tomorrow, both of you boys will report there after school on Tuesdays and Thursdays, plus every other Saturday. You'll learn about all the vehicles this family owns and anything else Dirk asks you to do. This isn't a request—this is your duty as superheroes. This is how you'll help us fight the Johnsons." Dad finished his speech with a shake of a fist.

Benny's voice sounded weak. "The battles aren't even dangerous," he pleaded.

"I'm sorry, son." I knew Dad meant it.

Benny fled the room. Dad and Mom looked at me. If they'd told me this a week ago I would have felt exactly like Benny—angry, frustrated, and disappointed. But my understanding of the world had been turned upside down. Something else was going on—something that was more important than battles.

"I'll talk to him," I said.

I found my brother on his bed, facedown in his pillow.

"Benny," I said.

"This is our chance," his voice was muffled. "It's finally our chance to be real heroes."

"You're already a hero," I said.

"What do you mean?" he asked.

I couldn't help but smile. "Aren't you the one who was going to stand up to a Super-super in the school library with nothing more than a jack-in-the-box belly button?"

Benny didn't move.

"Do you believe Juanita?" I asked. "Or do you think she's lying?"

Benny rolled over. "I don't know. It seems like she's telling the truth. What do you think?"

"I think I'm missing something," I said. "Something obvious."

"If she is telling the truth, and our families stop fighting . . ."

I finally understood. "Then you'll never get to go to a battle."

Benny nodded.

"Why don't you drop and give me fifty?" I said.

Benny snorted. "I can only do sixteen," he said.

"Then drop and give me sixteen," I said, smiling.

Benny sat up on the bed, his head hanging. I didn't have to imagine my brother's disappointment because I felt the same way.

Benny pushed himself off the bed and knelt on the floor. He stared at the carpet for a few moments, then raised his head to look at me. "One way or another, I'm going to get my supersuit," he said. "And when I do, I'm going to challenge Grandpa to a push-up contest. And I'm going to beat him."

I watched Benny do his push-ups, and moved the pieces to the puzzle around in my head.

15

I'VE ALWAYS WANTED TO TRY BROCCOLI

"Open the hatch up more," Dad called from below. "I can't find my spork."

"Your what?" I gasped. The hatch leading out from our root cellar was heavy. Brown stalks of weeds poked out of the snow. The ravine was deep, so we couldn't be seen from the road or any of the houses near by. I adjusted my feet, trying to get a better grip on the metal.

"Dad lost his spork," Benny called from below. "His flashlight is dead and he can't find it. He needs more light."

My feet slipped and the hatch closed with a thump. I landed on my backside and thought about getting up and opening it again, but it felt good to just lie there. Dad was a superhero. He'd figure out some way to find and rescue his spork.

A few minutes later the hatch opened up and Benny and Dad climbed out.

"That was some quick thinking, son," Dad said, holding up a gleaming titanium spork. "Once you closed the hatch, I could use my infrared goggles. Spork found. Crisis averted."

"What do you need your spork for, anyway?" I asked.

"It's all-you-can-eat sushi at Herman's Diner," Dad said. "Superheroes get a fifteen percent discount, and I prefer to eat my sushi with a spork."

Dad pulled Benny and me together, and then put his arms around us. "Going up!" he said.

Benny, Dad, and I shot into the air. It was after school on Thursday, and we were headed to the ranch.

Dad flew straight up before veering to the north. We soared over the suburbs of Split Rock, then downtown Split Rock, and then over more suburbs. He flew over the dump and around the new cell tower a few times, just to show off. When the cold became too much to bear, I pulled the hood of my coat down to protect my face from the biting wind.

Eventually the suburbs gave way to open fields blanketed in snow, then finally to wide-open spaces covered with sagebrush, scrub oak, and the occasional pine tree. Dad flew low to scare a few deer. They jumped and darted away.

Dad slowed, and I could see Grandpa's ranch as we descended, sitting there at the base of the small mountain we called Gunsight Peak. When I was little, I thought Grandpa was a humble rancher, trying to dry farm a few acres up one of the canyons north of the city.

After I learned the family secret, I discovered Grandpa owned the entire mountain, as well as a sprawling cavern underneath. I'm not sure how, but apparently superheroes make a lot of money without much effort.

Dad landed on the front lawn. "Nothing like a brisk afternoon flight around the city, eh, boys?" Dad said. "It really gets the blood pumping!"

We walked to the door, my shoes crunching in the frozen snow. Dad rang the doorbell, then stepped back off the porch. "I'll be back by seven," he said. He crouched, leaped into the air, and was gone.

"I hope Grandpa's here," Benny said. "Or we'll be stuck outside for three hours."

Grandpa was home. He opened the door a few moments later, his voice boisterous as he said, "Boys, come on in! Glad to see you made it."

I followed Benny inside the tidy home. A simple rug. An afghan on top of a weathered leather couch. Nothing hinted that the humble abode was really the headquarters for a family of superheroes.

"Do you boys need an after-school snack?" Grandpa held up a glass of milk. "This creamy goodness was in the goat just thirty minutes ago."

"No thanks, Grandpa." If you've ever had warm goat's milk, you know why I politely declined. It's kind of like throwing up in reverse.

"That's what's wrong with kids these days," Grandpa said. "When I was your age, I never turned down free food. How're you going to put any muscle on those bones if you don't drink your goat's milk?"

Grandpa finished off the milk, his mustache dripping with white froth. He gave an exaggerated sigh. "All right, enough lollygagging, let's get you two to Dirk." He rubbed his hands together and led me and Benny through the kitchen and out to the backyard.

"How're you boys holding up?" Grandpa said as we walked through the snow toward the base of the mountain.

"Well, we're here to work in the motor pool instead of getting our supersuits and going to battles," Benny said. "Does that answer your question?"

"Benny's been doing push-ups," I said, hoping to change the subject. "He did twenty last night."

"When I was your age, I could do about a thousand push-ups," Grandpa said. "Then I got my power, and I could do a million. Kind of boring doing a million, though. And nobody wants to sit there and watch." Grandpa looked at me. "What about you, Rafter? You doing all right?"

"I'm doing okay," I said. "Although there's something I wanted to ask you about."

"Fire away," Grandpa said. "If I know the answer I'll tell you. If I don't, I'll make something up."

"Benny and I were at the store with Dad on Tuesday," I said. "You know, where the battle took place?"

Grandpa nodded. "I heard that battle was a doozy. Wish I could've been there."

"The thing is, I don't think the Johnsons were doing anything. I mean, other than shopping. At least, not at first."

"They get to eat broccoli," Benny said. "I've always wanted to try broccoli. It looks like little trees."

"Trust me," Grandpa said. "Broccoli doesn't taste as good as it looks." Grandpa put his arm around me. "I doubt the Johnsons were just shopping." Grandpa shook his fist, then returned his arm to my shoulder. "Supervillains don't shop. They steal. They were up to something. If it involved broccoli, then that's a red flag right there."

I decided to get right to the point. "Grandpa, what do you think about sitting down and talking with the John-sons? You know, trying to come up with a truce?"

"You can't negotiate with supervillains," Grandpa said. "Even if they would sit down and talk, how could we agree on anything? We want what is best for this city. They just want to destroy it."

"Do you know that for sure?" I asked. "If you've never sat down to talk with them, how do you know what they want?"

"We've tried talking with them before," Grandpa said. "The Johnsons won't have anything to do with us." He shook his fist.

"You've tried?" I asked.

Grandpa nodded. "Several times that I can remember. Once we tried working through the mayor. And once the governor even got involved. But it seems like just when we start making progress, everything breaks down."

"Why do you have to go through somebody else?" I said. "Why not just call up the Johnsons directly?"

"Oh, you can't do that," Grandpa said. "You have to have a third party in these kinds of talks. Neither side can know where you're going to gather together until just a few hours before the meeting. Otherwise, you might be walking into an ambush."

My head felt like it was spinning. The Baileys were willing to talk. The Johnsons were willing to talk. So why hadn't the talks ever happened? I bet that Oscar Redding guy who sent the emails would know.

Grandpa stopped in front of an old-style outhouse

under a large oak tree. He reached forward and opened the door. "Skunks!" he shouted, and I jumped. Three skunks scurried around the inside of the outhouse.

"Dang it," I said. "Don't scare me like that!"

"Herman! Gladys! Loolah!" Benny shouted, leaning over to pet the black and white animals. "I love these skunks!"

Grandpa had some pretty tight security out at his ranch, but he also believed in simple measures. He said a few well-placed skunks were much better than any sophisticated alarm system. The skunks couldn't spray, so they were more or less harmless.

Grandpa stepped into the outhouse, and Benny and I followed. Benny shooed the skunks outside and Grandpa closed the door.

"Good thing this is a two-seater!" Grandpa said. He made that joke every time I'd ever been out here.

I'd only been out to the headquarters about a dozen times. I'd never visited the motor pool. In fact, I hadn't visited a lot of the places that were hidden under the mountain.

Pulling the toilet-paper dispenser off the wall revealed a panel with a touchpad. Grandpa pushed a few buttons, and the toilet dropped into the floor. A door opened up at the back of the outhouse, and all three of us stepped into an elevator. The door closed, and the elevator began to shake, first dropping us below ground, then carrying us horizontally into the heart of the mountain.

"Okay," Grandpa said, "You remember your cousin Dirk, right?"

I nodded. Dirk was twenty-three years old, born without legs below the knees. He was pretty much a super-engineer. He understood anything and everything about physics. I could never figure out how a guy like Dirk worked in the motor pool, and yet all we ever drove were beat-up cars that didn't really do anything special.

"Now remember," Grandpa said. "Dirk is a little . . . *particular* about his vehicles. But if you pay attention, you can learn a lot from that man."

"I'm glad he's particular about the vehicles, because nobody else wants to be," I muttered under my breath.

The elevator came to a stop. The doors opened, and for a moment I thought somebody was pulling a trick.

I'd expected a dingy room, cluttered with spare parts and old vehicles that Dirk tried to keep limping along.

It was nothing like that.

"Holy avocado buckets!" Benny said, stepping out of the elevator. I followed him, looking around and trying to take everything in.

The motor pool filled a sprawling warehouse. The walls and floor were stainless steel. Bright lights overhead emanated a soft, high-pitched hum. Dirk sat at a table holding a small set of pliers in one hand and a circuit board in the other. Behind him were rows and rows of the most incredible machines I'd ever seen—forest-green metal, polished black rubber, and chrome as far as the eye could see.

Cars, motorcycles, and Jeeps lined the left side of the room. Several Jet Skis, boats, two doughnut-shaped vehicles that I assumed were hovercrafts, and a small yacht sat in the back. To the right were two helicopters, a propeller plane, several personal aircrafts, and a small jet. In the middle of the room stood more cars, bikes, a tank, and something that looked like a miniature submarine.

"This is the coolest place ever," Benny said, his voice reverent. For the first time since the "surprise" meeting, I heard hope in my brother's voice.

Out of the corner of my eye, I saw Dirk smile. He put down the circuit board he'd been working on and stood. He was wearing shorts and his prosthetic legs, fashioned from some type of gleaming metal, were bent in a curved S shape and made a clicking sound when he walked.

Grandpa gave Benny and me a whack on the shoulders, then stepped back into the elevator. "Good luck, boys, I'll see you in a few hours. Work up an appetite. I'm milking Sandy again for dinner."

The door closed behind me but I barely noticed.

"How does . . . Where did we . . ." I couldn't even form a coherent question. I just waved at the vehicles and then looked at my cousin.

Dirk stopped in front of Benny and me and folded his arms. His smile grew bigger.

"You boys have just been let in on a little family secret," he said. "I've been designing, building, and testing these vehicles for about six years. Your brother Rodney has been helping me out on the technical side of things."

"Why don't we ever use these?" Benny asked. "Why are we always driving around in clunkers?"

"Well, for starters, we haven't worked out all of the kinks," Dirk said. "Some of these machines are still in the prototype stage. But the main reason is we don't want the Johnsons to know. We're building a fleet of vehicles that will be able to run circles around anything they have. When we're ready to show them what we've got, it'll be years before they can catch up."

I remembered the barking robotic dog at Juanita's headquarters. Sure, they had a cute barking puppy that could pop bubbles. We had an entire room filled with armored vehicles. If we really wanted to, we could take out the Johnsons at any time.

I had a whole new appreciation for working in the motor pool—to climb into one of these vehicles and sit behind the wheel. Or the stick. Or whatever you used to steer some of these machines. With a sudden desire to feel cold metal under my fingers, I stepped forward.

"Hold it right there, partner." Dirk grabbed me by the

back of my sweater. He had a lean face and it was clear he hadn't shaved in a few days. "A few rules," he said, smiling. "You listening up?"

I nodded.

"Eyes on me," Dirk replied. "Not the machines."

I forced my gaze away from the shiny temptations.

"This is my room," Dirk said. His voice was firm but kind. "I'm responsible for every piece of equipment this family owns. These machines have to be in tip-top shape when the family needs them, understand?"

Benny and I nodded.

Dirk continued. "I can't have two kids running around messing things up, got it?"

At the word *kids*, my heart sank. I wondered if Dirk even wanted us here.

"Notice the red line." Dirk pointed to a thick red line that made a large square surrounding the elevator door. Two desks sat on one side, inside the square. We were on the inside of the square, too. The vehicles were all on the outside.

"You don't cross that line until you've completed my training," Dirk said. "Understand?"

Benny and I nodded.

"No exceptions," Dirk said. "If I'm working on a car, and it falls on top of me, and I'm trapped underneath it, you stay on this side of the line. Got it?"

That sounded a bit extreme, but I nodded again.

"Notice your study area." Dirk pointed at the two desks. "That's where you'll read and learn. If you study hard, you can pass my test. Once you pass my test"—Dirk pointed to the line again—"you can cross the line."

I had a sneaking suspicion that the test wasn't going to be easy.

Dirk pointed behind us. "Notice the bookcases."

I turned and looked. Eight bookcases filled with books, manuals, and stacks of bound paper stood against the wall. There were two desks next to the bookcases.

"Those books contain the information you'll need to pass my test," Dirk said. "It's not as hard as you think. If you've got half a brain, you'll be able to pass the test in two, three years tops." Dirk took a step back and looked us up and down, his smile teasing. "Maybe four years."

"Wait a minute," Benny said. "Just so I'm clear on this. If we study hard for four years, and pass your test, then and only then we'll be able to drive these vehicles?"

Dirk shook his head. "I'm sorry—sometimes I don't communicate very well. If you study hard for four years, then you'll be able to cross the line. That allows you to crack open the hoods and start working on these babies. You can't drive any of these machines until you have your SVDL—that stands for *specialized vehicle driver's license*. And you can't get that until you're twenty-one."

"Twenty-one?" Benny said, his voice filled with disbelief. "So I can't drive these things for . . ." He counted on his fingers. "Nine years? That's almost as long as I've been alive!"

"Actually," Dirk explained, "you can't drive anything with a weapons system until you're twenty-*three*. At least not on the road. Insurance reasons, I think."

"How many of them have a weapons system?" I asked, though I'd already guessed the answer.

Dirk smiled, and I thought I saw a hint of sympathy in my cousin's face. "All of them. Though sometimes we remove the weapons if we need stealth. So in those situations, you can drive them when you're twenty-one."

Dirk clapped his hands. "Okay, you'll find the manuals to each of the machines in the first two bookcases. Books about engines are in the third, transmissions in the fourth, auxiliary and weapons in the next two, and the rest of the books cover mechanical history, design, mathematics, engineering, and physics." He pointed at the desks. "You boys will start on something simple. I want a report on the history and purpose of the glove compartment by the end of the month."

"The what?" I asked. "You want a report on what?"

"Isn't the purpose of the glove compartment to store gloves?" Benny asked.

"Or is it?" Dirk said, raising his eyebrows.

Dirk turned and walked back to the table, his metal feet clicking on the floor.

Silence settled over the room. Benny walked over to one of the desks and dropped heavily in the chair. Somewhere a fan turned on.

I went over to the other desk and steadied myself against it. My knees felt weak.

I was done. I was tired, I was angry, and I was done.

Boats. Assault vehicles. Aircraft. I was surrounded by a world of technology, action, and adventure. And I had no place in it. I couldn't even cross the line to feel the adventure with my fingertips.

Right at that moment I saw the truth. I saw the truth and I hated it.

I would never save the day. I would never solve the problem of the feuding families. I wasn't a superhero, and I never would be.

I was nothing.

Pulling out a chair, I sat down at a desk. I could feel the hot sting of tears in my eyes. I looked down at the floor. I didn't want this. I didn't want to be in the world of superheroes if I couldn't be *part* of that world.

I would run away. I would find a new place to live where there weren't any Baileys or Johnsons or saving the day. Where a kid could get a B+ on his algebra exam and that would be enough.

Benny sniffled to my left. I looked over and my heart broke.

My younger brother sat hunched over his own desk, head hanging down. His eyes were red. He wiped tears off his cheeks with the back of one hand. In the other hand, he held a book. I saw the title of the book and my stomach dropped.

A Brief History of Glove Compartments.

I let the low burn of anger in my gut grow.

Life had kicked me and Benny to the curb. Told us we were worthless. And how did Benny respond? By standing up, shaking off the dust, and studying glove compartments. As if nothing had happened.

Nothing could stop Benny.

I felt my anger growing and turned it to determination. If my little brother could keep fighting, then so could I.

Oscar Redding had tried to do something important. He'd tried to do the impossible—to get two superfamilies to stop fighting.

I pulled open my phone and typed in a message to Rodney.

Send me anything you can find on Oscar Redding.

16

I DON'T THINK THAT'S EVEN CORRECT GRAMMAR

"Come on, Rodney, tell me what you've found," I said.

"Can't stop. In a groove." Rodney stopped typing long enough to drain a glass of goat's milk, then started up again.

I sat next to my brother, watching him work. He was sitting in front of four monitors, each streaming information that made no sense to me. He loved a challenge and had started doing research yesterday as soon as I'd asked him.

I flipped through a stack of papers in front of me. One of them was an email from Oscar Redding to our family, just like the one he'd sent the Johnsons. Like Benny said, it made sense. We'd destroyed his factory during one of our battles, so he wanted to get the families to stop fighting. From what I could tell, Oscar worked with the Johnsons until they'd agreed to meet with our family. Then Oscar had contacted Grandpa. Grandpa had discussed it with the family and said we were willing to talk, but Oscar never wrote back. He'd worked so hard to get the families to meet, and then for some reason he just dropped the whole issue.

I wanted to find out everything I could about this man, but so far my research had been turning up dead ends. That's when I remembered the citizen who Juanita said called her family in the first place. Where did that citizen get his information, anyway? And what about the citizen who had called us?

I asked Rodney if he could track the phone number and Rodney boasted he'd have it for me in less than five minutes. That was forty-five minutes ago. He was still looking.

My brother stopped typing, but it was only to push his glasses farther up his nose. He scowled at the screen. "Oh, you think a triple-cross transatlantic relay pattern is going to stop me?" Rodney said to his computer. "Well, that's child's play, my friend. Do you hear me? Child's play." He started typing again.

"Do you think you'll be able to find it?" I asked.

Rodney stopped and looked over his glasses at me. "Please, Rafter. It's me you're talking to."

He went back to work.

A speaker on the desk crackled to life. "Rodney? Rafter? It's dinnertime. Come and get it while it's cold."

That was Mom's little joke. It seemed like every other night we had cold mashed potatoes and chard for dinner. Another superhero diet staple.

I pressed a button on the speaker. "We'll be right up, Mom."

Rodney tapped the return key and stared at the screen.

"And . . . there we have it." He pointed at the monitor. *October J.*

"That's who owns the phone that called in the robbery on the White Knight," Rodney said. "October Johnson. You know what this means, right, Rafter?"

I had no idea what it meant.

"You have cracked the problem that has been plaguing us for years."

"What problem is that?" I didn't feel like I'd cracked anything.

"The Johnsons usually only send four people to the battles," Rodney said. "We usually have six to eight, and yet they still manage to win half the time." He tapped the screen. "This is why."

"I still don't get it," I admitted. "The J. doesn't have to

stand for Johnson. Maybe it stands for something else."

Rodney ignored me. "They know where the battles are going to be ahead of time. It's like having home court advantage. They decide where they want to fight, and then they call us up and we go running. That's why we struggle even though we have more people."

I wasn't convinced. "Maybe."

Rodney flicked the power switch and headed upstairs. I followed. I stopped on the third stair from the top. If Rodney was right, then that meant Juanita had been lying. Not about everything—I really did believe she had a worthless power now—but maybe she wasn't giving us the *whole* truth. But once again I felt the nagging sensation that I was missing something. A key piece of information.

Tactics.

Something tickled the back of my brain. Why did Oscar Redding stop trying to reconcile the families? That seemed to be crucial.

If I could just figure that piece of the puzzle out, I was convinced the rest would fall into place.

Mom, Rodney, and Benny were already at the table. Dad brought over bowls of cold mashed potatoes, chard, and lime wedges. I dished up food and pushed it around on my plate.

"Why do we have to eat this stuff again?" I asked.

"Superheroes have always eaten this food, sweetie,"

Mom said. "It gives us energy to fight the Johnsons." She shook her fist.

A week ago I might have accepted that answer. "Benny and I don't get to fight the Johnsons. We get to work in the motor pool. I think we should get to eat burgers and french fries."

Dad changed the subject. "How was your first day of training?" Dad asked, dumping mashed potatoes onto his plate.

"Training's fine," Benny said.

"What's Dirk got you studying? Flamethrowers? The modified 1942 army Jeep? Or what about the grappling hook on the hovercraft? When you hook that baby up to a helicopter all sorts of fun stuff happens."

"Glove compartments," Benny said.

"Glove compartments?" Dad asked.

"Glove compartments," Benny replied.

Dad looked puzzled. "Really? That doesn't seem like the most exciting place to start. I mean, I guess the glove compartment is important if you're not quite sure where to store your gloves, but . . . you boys know where to store gloves, right?"

"Feel free to bring the matter up with Dirk," I said. "I'd be more than happy to start with something more exciting."

"Oh, no," Dad said, shaking his head. "Dirk knows his machines. If he started you on the glove compartment, then that's the best place to start."

"Did you know," Benny said, "that a T9 reinforced glove compartment, once properly secured, can contain an explosion of up to two-point-seven sticks of dynamite without hurting the rest of the car?" Benny had really been studying that book.

"That's interesting," Dad said, although it was clear from his tone that he didn't think it was.

"The only thing I don't get," Benny said, "is that I don't think you'd often have two-point-seven sticks of dynamite lit at the same time. It seems like you'd either have two sticks, or three sticks, but not two-point-seven. I guess if you had three sticks, you could always cut off part of one of the sticks before you put it in the glove compartment. But then again, if the sticks were already lit, I'd just drop them and run. I don't think cutting up dynamite is such a good idea."

"Little brother," Rodney said. "You've succeeded in making this the most boring dinner conversation of all time."

Benny wasn't through. "What do you think would happen if you put three sticks in the glove compartment? Would it completely destroy the car, or would it just do point-three sticks' worth of damage?"

"Well, I suppose it would . . ." Dad clearly had no interest in glove compartments.

"I guess if you had some really good scissors, you could cut the dynamite," Benny said. "But scissors aren't standard on the utility belts. I guess you could bite the dynamite, but if the dynamite went off when you were biting? I'd hate to have to explain that to the dentist."

The dentist.

For some reason my mind seized on that word like it was important.

Suddenly I felt a vibration in my pocket. At the same time, I heard a buzz from across the table. And two chimes. And a chicken cluck. All at once, everybody was reaching into their pockets.

I dug out my phone, and read the message on the screen.

Who will be left to save the day when all the heroes are gone? —With love, The Johnsons.

"What is this nonsense?" Dad said. "I don't think that's even correct grammar. Shouldn't it be *whom*?"

I rubbed at my ears. "Can anybody else hear that humming?" I asked. An electronic squealing noise filled the air. It came from outside, and it was getting higher and higher in pitch.

"I don't hear anything," Dad said.

Neither did Mom, but Benny and Rodney both did.

I stood and moved to the window. The noise was getting painful. From where I stood I could see the lights of downtown. The sprawling suburbs. And then a flash. At first it was a pinprick, almost like a single star close to the horizon. And then the lightning flared into the sky. Not from the sky—*into* the sky. The lightning came from the pinprick of light, east of downtown.

The night erupted into bright white light.

17

TO THE MITSUBISHI!

My eyes were still trying to adjust to the flash when a wave of thunder crashed over the house, shaking walls, rattling Mom's hanging-forks decoration, and vibrating the floorboards under my feet.

When the house settled down, Dad asked, "Is everyone all right?"

I let go of the windowsill. The sky was dark and quiet once again.

I nodded.

"Was that lightning?" Benny asked.

"Not lightning like I've ever seen before," I said. "It looked like it shot up from the ground."

Dad wiped his mouth with his napkin. "Clearly the

Johnsons are up to something," he said. "I'm changing into my suit." Dad left the room.

"Something isn't right," Rodney said. "It's like I was in the middle of doing something, and I didn't quite finish. Like I've left something undone."

"I feel the same way," Mom said.

We sat in awkward silence until Dad came back into the room, dressed in his supersuit. "I'm off to see Grandpa," he said. "We'll find out what is going on." He strode to the window and looked out. "It's dark enough that I don't think anybody will see me fly out this way. Stay here and don't answer the door."

Dad opened the window and jumped. I heard a crash.

"GAH!"

I went to the window. Dad was lying facedown on the frozen ground of the flower garden. His arms stretched out in front of him.

"What're you doing?" I asked. And then it hit me.

The flash of light.

Just like the one I'd seen on the day Benny and I got our powers.

I turned and saw Rodney still in a daze.

"Rodney," I said. "Have you lost your power?"

Rodney looked stunned. "That's it," he said. "I'm . . . I'm not smart anymore. I have a brain the size of . . . of a pea." His voice filled with panic. "I'm like a *Tyrannosaurus rex*, with a tiny little pea-brain. Like a chickpea. Have you ever seen a chickpea, Rafter?"

Minutes before he'd been downstairs racing through the internet, fingers flying, tracking down a supervillain. And now . . .

"You're still smart, Rodney," I said, trying to sound encouraging. "You knew that a *T. rex* has a brain the size of a chickpea. That's something, right?"

"That's just it," Rodney said slowly. He seemed to be in a daze. "I'm not sure about the whole chickpea thing. It might be a walnut. I can't remember because I've lost all my brain power."

"Do you have a new power?" I asked.

Rodney looked at me and nodded. "Yes. Yes, I do." He lifted up his hands. "I can stop my fingernails from growing." He paused, then spoke again. "See? They're not growing. Right now, they've stopped growing."

"Mom?" I asked. "What about you?"

Mom didn't say anything for a few seconds. Then she said, "I can play an accordion with one hand."

The front door slammed, and Dad walked in. He had snow and mud smeared over the front of his suit. "I don't mean to alarm anybody, but I can't fly."

Dad looked surprised that none of us looked surprised.

"That flash of light gave everybody worthless powers," I said. "Do you have a worthless power?"

Dad cocked his head to the side. I could see him searching his brain for his new power. He opened his mouth and burped.

"Смотрите, что я умею."

"It appears I can burp in Russian," Dad said. His phone rang and he answered it. Benny looked at me, his eyebrows raised. I shrugged my shoulders.

"Well, that changes nothing," Dad said into the phone. "Of course we'll come. Right. Good-bye."

Dad closed his phone. "That was Grandpa. It appears all of the Baileys in Split Rock have lost their powers. Reports are coming in that the Johnsons are waging a full-scale attack. They were last seen heading toward the stadium."

"What does Grandpa want us to do?" Rodney asked.

"Grandpa said it was probably safest to get out of the city," Dad said. "But that's not what he's going to do. And it's not what I'm going to do either. I'm going to meet the supervillains at the stadium, with or without my powers."

Rodney stood. "I'm coming with you. Without my real power I'm no good down in the root cellar. I'll get my suit."

Mom got up and left the room as well.

Benny looked over at me. I could read the look on his face as clearly as if he was shouting. He wanted to go to the battle, but I shook my head. I had other plans, and I needed Benny's help. It didn't even seem to occur to Dad that we might come along. Even when all our powers were equally worthless, Dad still saw Benny and me as little kids.

Mom and Rodney walked back into the room, dressed in their suits.

"We can't fly, so we'll have to take the car," Dad said. And then, in his booming superhero voice, he said, "To the Mitsubishi!"

I followed them out to the garage. They piled into our car and the engine roared to life.

"Dad," I called out. "Be careful. Something isn't right."

Dad nodded, then backed the car out of the garage and was gone.

Benny stood there, folding his arms. "Once again, we're left sitting at home. And this time we don't even get to watch the battle on the monitors."

"We're not going to sit at home," I said. "Not this time."

"Really?" Benny asked. "What are we going to do?"

I pulled up the message that Juanita had sent me the day of the supermarket battle. I hit reply, and typed a quick message.

Meet us at Callahan Park. Ten minutes.

"We're going to talk to Juanita," I said. "And we're going to solve this puzzle, once and for all."

18

IT'S THE ONLY DAY OF THE YEAR WE GET TO EAT CARAMEL

I stood in Callahan Park, my bike leaning against a tree. Benny sat on his bike, his feet planted on the ground. He had a backpack slung over his shoulders. He'd insisted on bringing some necessities, just in case. He had duct tape, rope, and a flashlight. *Superhero essentials*, he'd said.

I paced in front of the tree, trying to straighten things out in my mind.

"There's Juanita," Benny said. "Wow, she can ride pretty fast."

Juanita rode like an invisible Aunt Verna was chasing her. She jerked the bike from side to side as she pedaled. When Juanita got within ten feet of Benny and me, she jumped off her bike, threw her helmet to the ground, and tackled me. In another second she was sitting on my chest, and had both my arms pinned to the ground with her knees.

It wasn't quite the greeting I expected.

"What did you do to my family?" Juanita yelled. She brought up her fists. "Tell me or you're about to meet my two good friends, pain and suffering."

I don't do my best thinking when somebody is threatening me with bodily harm. "Juanita," I said in a weak voice—weak because I found it difficult to breathe with her sitting on my chest. "What are you talking about?"

Juanita grabbed me by the front of my coat and brought her face close to mine. "Don't you lie to me, Rafter Bailey," she said. She spit over her left shoulder, and then pushed her face back into mine. "I bring you into our headquarters. I trust you. And then tonight I get a text message from your family asking who would save the day if there were no more heroes. Then there's a flash of light, and my dad has a worthless power." She let go of my coat, and I fell back to the frozen dirt.

"Do you mean . . ." The light. Oscar Redding. The dentist. October J. The puzzle pieces in my mind shifted and moved . . . and then fell into place.

And just like that, I had the answer.

"Juanita," I said. "Get off me."

She didn't move.

"Please," I said.

She must have heard the desperation in my voice. She stood and I got up.

"You don't look so good, Rafter," Benny said. "You look like you need a Benny bag."

"Benny," I said, still gasping for air. "You know how Uncle Ralph hauls his family off for dentist appointments in November and April, right?"

"Yeah," said Benny. "He says the best time to get a teeth cleaning is after Halloween, and after the Tax Day Caramel Fest."

"The Tax Day what?" Juanita asked.

"It's the only day of the year we get to eat caramel," Benny explained.

"That's not important," I said. "Benny, do you remember back in the school library? You were talking about the battle at the thermal underwear factory—Oscar Redding's factory. We beat the Johnsons even though Uncle Henry and his family were at the dentist. That means we fought the battle in November. Don't you see what that means?" I stopped and looked at my brother and Juanita.

They returned my stares with blank looks.

"Oscar Redding didn't call for an end to the battles because we destroyed his factory," I explained. "He called an end to the battles *before* we destroyed it."

"Oh, I see!" Benny paused, and then said, "Wait, no I don't."

I looked at Juanita. She shrugged. "I'm lost too."

It was so clear in my mind. "Oscar Redding tried all last summer to get the families together. To get us to sit down and work out our differences. He's a powerful man, and maybe people started listening. Maybe people out there are a little tired of us destroying their property, or arresting them for silly things. And what happens next?" I answered my own question. "Somebody destroys his factory."

"It wasn't somebody," Benny said. "It was us."

I shook my head. "No. Somebody called up our family and told us the Johnsons were smuggling weapons into the country." I pointed at Juanita. "And then somebody called up your family and told you we were building a laser. Whoever that somebody was, they used us like a guided missile to destroy Oscar Redding's factory."

Juanita gasped. She saw it.

"I am so lost," Benny said. "You're going to have to spell it out for me."

"Somebody wanted to stop Oscar Redding," Juanita said. "Just like they've stopped the mayor, and the governor, and who knows who else? They don't want peace between the families."

"Right," I said. "They probably threatened him. They told him if he didn't stop, something bad would happen.

Oscar Redding didn't back down, so they destroyed his factory. The same person probably threatened anyone who calls for peace between the families."

Benny looked confused. "But who would do something like that?"

"The same person who has gone to so much trouble to keep us fighting in the first place," I said. "The same person who wants to keep us busy so he can do whatever he wants."

Benny's eyes got wide, and he leaned in close. "Is it the librarian? I've *always* suspected that guy."

"Mr. Wells?" I had no idea where Benny came up with that one. "No. It's not the librarian."

"Then who?" Benny asked.

Juanita spoke before I could. I thought I heard the same hint of fear in her voice as I felt in my stomach.

"A supervillain," she said. "The real supervillain."

I nodded. "Rodney tracked down a name. October J. I'll bet my supersuit that—"

"You can't bet your supersuit," Benny said. "You don't have one yet. And neither do—"

"My family!" Juanita screamed. She pulled out her phone.

"What is it?" I asked.

"My dad got a call right after he lost his power," Juanita said. She finished typing on the phone and held it to her ear. "My entire family left to go to the stadium. To fight with your family."

"I don't understand—" I started, and then I did.

All of the superheroes in the city, gathered together in one place.

Without powers.

I pulled out my phone just as I heard Juanita talking into hers. I dialed Dad's number. After what seemed like three incredibly long rings, Dad answered. "Rafter? Is that you?"

"Dad, you can't go to the stadium."

"What are you talking about? We're almost there."

"Dad, it's a trap."

"It doesn't matter," Dad said. "Someone has to stand up to the Johnsons. With or without powers, it's going to be the Baileys."

For once in my life I wished my Dad wasn't so super.

I heard Juanita say, "First Dam" into the phone.

"Dad, the Johnsons aren't going to the stadium anymore. They're going to First Dam."

"How do you know?" Dad asked.

"There isn't any time to explain, Dad. But you have to believe me." I looked over at Juanita who had already hung up. She nodded. I spoke into the phone. "The Johnsons are heading to First Dam."

There was a pause. "Rafter . . . are you sure?"

"Yes, Dad," I replied. "I'm sure."

There was static on the other end of the line, and I could almost hear Dad trying to decide. "Okay, we'll head over there now. Thanks for the heads up, Rafter. Good work."

I let out a sigh and hung up the phone. I opened the Bailey Family Locater app. Dad was true to his word. One by one, the dots that represented the members of my family were turning toward the east—toward the canyon and First Dam.

I closed the phone and said to Juanita, "That was good thinking."

Juanita put her helmet on and picked up her bike. "Thanks," she said.

"Wait," I said. "Where are you going?"

"Home," Juanita said. "Our families are safe . . . at least for now. When my dad gets home, I'll tell him about the supervillain."

I chose my next words carefully. "Juanita. Somewhere out there is a real supervillain. This supervillain stole our powers, along with the rest of our families'. If we can find him, we could get our powers back. Our real powers."

Juanita stared at me. "You want me to ride out into the night and fight with a supervillain? With the two of you?"

The way she said it did make it sound a little silly.

"I don't know that we'll have to actually fight him," I said. "But if we can find proof that he's out there, we'd still need your help to convince your family. Then maybe both our families could team up."

Juanita just stood there, atop her bike.

"I was looking out of the window when the light flashed," I said. "At the beginning there was this ball of lightning. I can't be sure, but it looked to me like it might be close to the city dump. Or even *in* the city dump."

Juanita sighed. Her shoulders slumped, and it looked like she'd just run a marathon. "Listen, I think it's great you guys want to be super. I really do. But I don't want anything to do with this. I never wanted to be super."

Your mother saved the lives of three people, I wanted to say.

"I'm not asking you be super," I said. "But right now there are people in trouble. Your family. My family. And if all of the superheroes lose their powers, this supervillain will be able to do anything. Innocent citizens could be in danger. People could get hurt."

Juanita looked at the ground. Her hair covered her face so I couldn't see it. I waited.

"We could really use your help," Benny said.

Juanita didn't move. I saw the sharp point of a crescent moon rising above the mountain behind her. Somewhere a piece of frozen snow broke loose from a branch and fell to the ground.

Juanita raised her head. "I'll come," she said. "Because people are in danger."

I nodded. "Thanks, Juanita."

Benny tightened his helmet. "Enough with the speeches," he said, his voice giddy. "It's time for action!"

With that, Benny was off. I grabbed my bike and followed. Juanita brought up the rear.

A thought went through my mind. One that sent a tingle up my spine. Somewhere out there, a villain had set a plan into motion. He'd been manipulating my family for years, and now he probably thought he was stealing candy from a baby.

But pedaling through the dark, blowing puffs of hot breath into the night air, three superheroes were about to fight back.

19

THIS IS NO ORDINARY GLOVE COMPARTMENT

The city dump wasn't hard to get to. We loaded our bikes on the 259 bus heading north. We got off at Lincoln, and then it was a short bike ride to the dump. The wind against my hands and face was bitter cold. When we were almost there, Benny was the first to spot the device.

"What is that?" he asked.

I looked where he pointed. At first I couldn't see anything special. And then I saw it, just above the mounds of garbage—a large white sphere, sitting atop the cell tower. It looked like a giant golf ball.

"Has that always been there?" Benny asked.

"I've never seen it before," Juanita said.

The gate to the dump was locked. We threw our bikes in the bushes and climbed the chain-link fence. As a law-abiding citizen I would never consider breaking and entering city property. But we were in superhero mode, and the superhero code allowed it.

As we got closer I could see the sphere better. It wasn't a smooth ball, but was made up of a lot of hexagons. It reminded me of a twenty-sided die.

"Should we call Dad?" Benny asked. "If we can get all the superheroes here, maybe we can figure out what's going on."

I weighed our options. "If we call Dad," I said, "and Juanita calls in the Johnsons, do you think they'll let us stay? Or will we just be the kids without the supersuits again?"

Benny didn't have to answer.

"Let's take a look around first," I said. "We can call in backup if we decide we need it."

Walls of garbage stood between the tower and us. "How do you think we get there?" I asked.

Juanita pulled out her phone and brought up a satellite map of the area. "This way," she said, and she was off and running. The whole thing looked like a maze to me, but Juanita seemed sure. She led us through piles of garbage and eventually came to a stop. I almost ran into her. It was a full minute before Benny came to a stop next to us, gasping.

"Doing push-ups does *not* help you run faster," he said when he finally caught his breath. "You guys didn't save the day without me, did you? Although technically I guess it would be saving the night."

I smiled in the darkness. "No. Nobody has saved the night. But that's what we're up against." I pointed.

At the base of the tower was a black van. About ten feet away was an old-style RV that looked like an enormous egg. It had a door and a window on the side facing us. The window was either dirty, foggy, or both. Someone moved around inside the RV.

Benny looked over at me and Juanita. "A van and an old RV? We can totally handle that. It's not even a cool van like the ones we have in our motor pool."

"I don't know," Juanita said to Benny. "I think you had it right the first time. I think we should call our families. Someone's moving around inside that RV." She pointed up at the white sphere. "Look at those scorch marks. And can you smell the sulfur in the air?"

From where we were standing, I could see black smudges against the white wall of the sphere.

"It smells like the time I tried to microwave an egg wrapped in tinfoil," Benny said.

I didn't want to watch somebody else save the day.

"The van's empty," I said. "You guys can call in backup if you want. I'm going to see who's in that RV."

I crept forward, my feet crunching on the ice. I heard Benny and Juanita follow. I started to make my way to the window of the RV when I saw the handle on the door turn.

I ran toward the front of the van, ducking down against the headlights. In a few seconds, Juanita and Benny were crouched beside me.

I heard the door to the RV swing open. I got down on my hands and knees and peered under the van in time to see boots step down from the RV and walk toward us. For a split second I pictured the owner of the boots getting into the van, starting it up, and shining his lights right in our eyes. But the boots went to the back of the van, then disappeared as the person climbed in through the trunk. I placed my hand on the front bumper and could feel the van shake as somebody moved around inside.

A minute passed. Then another. I heard the trunk door open and watched as the boots moved from the van back to the RV, then disappeared inside.

"Come on," I said, moving to the back of the van. I opened the door as quietly as I could and slipped inside. Benny and Juanita followed.

A dome light bathed the inside of the van in a dim yellow glow. The seats in the back had been stripped out, and the only windows were on the back doors. Metal shelves lined the walls. It felt more like a cage than a vehicle. Fast-food wrappers were scattered around the area. The van smelled like rancid grease.

The shelves and floor were covered with electronics—wires, circuit boards, cords . . . it looked like somebody had taken apart fifty computers and thrown them around in here.

"This looks like a supervillain's van to me," Benny said.

Juanita kicked a crumpled fast-food sack. Benny poked through the shelves in the back. I kept watch out the window to make sure nobody was coming. Juanita moved to the front of the vehicle.

"Look what I found," she whispered. In the dim light I couldn't see what she held up. Then the object in her palm was glowing.

"A phone?" Benny moved to look over Juanita's shoulder.

"That day we met in the library, I was headed home when this strange guy in pajamas, a stocking cap, and a trench coat stopped and pointed a phone at me."

"Did he have a fake beard?" Benny asked. "We saw the same guy, do you remember, Rafter?"

I nodded. "We thought he was a Johnson."

"Yeah," Juanita said. "And I thought he was a Bailey. But this phone looks exactly like what he was pointing at me."

I couldn't be sure, but I thought Juanita might be right. The phone looked familiar.

Juanita began flipping through screens. "Let's see what this thing can do."

I looked out the window again to make sure we were still alone.

Benny whispered from the front of the van. "Holy gravy. Will you look at that!"

I spun around, my heart thumping. "What is it? What's wrong?"

"Look at this glove compartment," Benny said.

"What?" I asked.

"He's got a T9 installed," Benny said. "I'd recognize a T9 anywhere."

Juanita, whose head had been bouncing back and forth between Benny and me like she was watching tennis, finally asked, "Your parents don't let you guys out much, do they?"

"This is no ordinary glove compartment," Benny said. "You can put up to two-point-seven sticks of dynamite in this baby, and there wouldn't be any—"

"Benny," I said. "Now is not the time or the place for a discussion on glove compartments. Why don't you look inside the glove compartment and see if you can find who owns this van?"

"Are you crazy?" Benny said. "You can't break into a T9. The only way we could get in there is if . . . oh. It's unlocked. Never mind."

"If we're right," I said, "this van will be owned by somebody named October. Last initial—J."

"October is such a funny name," Benny said as he shuffled through papers he'd pulled out of the glove compartment. Juanita continued to tap at the phone with a finger while I kept an eye out the back window.

"I found the registration," Benny whispered from the front. "It's not October. The guy who owns this van is named Charles. Charles Jones."

Jones. October J. October Jones.

I'm embarrassed it took me so long. We weren't dealing with a single supervillain. We were dealing with a whole other family.

Instead of three kids up against a single person, we were now three kids up against . . . who knows how many people?

I came to the uncomfortable realization that I was very likely way out of my league.

I looked back to Benny. "Okay," I said. "Benny, call Grandpa. Juanita, you call—"

Juanita sounded like she was in a daze. "I don't believe it," she said.

"What?" Benny and I said at the same time.

"When I saw the pajama man," Juanita said, "he pointed this device at me and then laughed. I figured the phone told him what my power was."

I'd guessed the same thing.

"But this does more than that." Juanita's eyes shined.

"This is *the* device. This controls that tower out there, which controls our powers. This thing can give a superhero worthless powers. Or we can use it to get our real powers back."

It took a moment to process what Juanita was saying. Our real powers. Juanita held our real powers in the palm of her hand.

"Juanita," I said, trying to keep my voice calm. "Are you telling me that all you have to do is push a few buttons, and we can finally be super?"

Juanita didn't have time to answer. The door opened behind me, and somebody grabbed the collar of my coat and dragged me out of the back of the van.

20

IT'S PROBABLY SAFE TO ASSUME YOU DON'T GET INVITED TO A LOT OF PARTIES

My feet slipped on the ice, and I fell to the ground. I watched as a man jumped inside the van. There were the sounds of a brief struggle, and then the man came back out holding the phone Juanita had shown us just a moment before.

It was Pajama Man—the same one who had confronted Benny and me in front of our school.

He wore the same stocking cap he'd had on when we saw him at school. He was tall and thin, with dark eyes that sat under fat and furry eyebrows. He wore heavy black boots and a thick coat.

Juanita squatted just inside the van. Benny came out the side door. He looked like he was ready for a fight.

I didn't think either one of them realized how much trouble we were in.

The henchman pushed a few buttons on the phone, and then slipped it into his pocket. "So, what kind of critters have infested my van?"

My hand edged toward the phone in my pocket.

"Come, come, my dear." The man motioned to Juanita through the back door. "It must be stuffy in there. Feel free to step out into the fragrant night air." The man spread out his hands and smiled. "I would introduce myself, but I think I prefer my anonymity."

I decided to press my luck. "You don't need to introduce yourself, Charles."

The man spun around to face me, his eyes becoming thin slits. "Where did you . . . how much do you know, boy?"

I said nothing. Let him wonder how much I knew. This was an especially good tactic since the sad truth was, I knew next to nothing.

"Well, it doesn't matter," Charles said, waving his hand. He turned to face Juanita. "Please, step outside."

I put my hand in my pocket, and grasped my phone. I tried to look casual.

Charles stood there, his arms folded, with an I-hate-you smile on his face. "It sounds like you three have been doing your homework. You've discovered something about our little family, have you? That's too bad. People don't live very long once they've met the Joneses."

Juanita looked surprised, but she recovered almost immediately. "Your family sounds like a cheery bunch," she said, climbing out of the van. "It's probably safe to assume you don't get invited to a lot of parties?"

"Pass me your phones," Charles said, snapping his fingers.

In an instant my brain formulated a plan. There were three of us. He couldn't catch us all at once.

"Run!" I shouted, pulling the phone out of my pocket. "Run and call for help."

It was a good plan. It should have worked. Only it didn't. One moment I was running, moving away from the van. The next moment, I wasn't moving at all. A brief moment of disorientation, and then nothing.

Looking down at my feet, I realized I was twelve inches off the ground.

I was flying.

21

I DON'T FEEL LIKE HOLDING HANDS RIGHT NOW

For a split second I thought I'd gotten my real power. That maybe Juanita had figured out how to use the special phone before Charles had stolen it from her. But the high-pitched laughter that pierced the air told me the truth. I wasn't flying at all.

I was trapped.

I waved my arms and kicked my legs. It felt like I was in zero gravity, and nothing I did helped me move.

I saw that Benny and Juanita were in the same predicament. Both hovered a foot off the ground. In a moment, Charles gathered up our phones and put them in his trench-coat pocket.

"You know," said Charles. "When I was a boy, I always wanted to fly. I wanted to soar over the trees and spit on people who were trapped on the ground. You can imagine my disappointment when I got a power that let me make everyone fly but myself." He shrugged. "But you find ways to use the power that's given to you."

Another bout of disorientation came over me as I rose higher into the air. I was six feet off the ground when Charles grabbed me by my pant leg. I tried to break loose, but his grip was too tight. He pulled me like a helium-filled balloon to the middle of a clearing surrounded by piles of trash. Then he went for Benny and Juanita.

I didn't like what I was seeing.

"You know, it's kind of sad how easy it was to keep your families fighting," Charles said as he grabbed Benny and pulled him toward me. "You're so concerned about looking heroic and fighting with the other family that you don't even notice the real threat to the city."

Charles left Benny hovering near me and then returned for Juanita.

I was ready to grasp at straws.

"I'm a little disappointed," I said. "We didn't come looking for some low-level henchman. We came looking for October Jones."

The villain looked at me sharply, then smiled. "My, my, you really are full of surprises. If there was any question about your fate, you just sealed it. Grandpa certainly won't want you around if you know his name."

Grandpa. October Jones. Leader of the Jones family— at least in Split Rock.

My stomach filled with ice.

Charles left Juanita hovering by Benny and me. "Why are you bothering with three kids who don't even have real superpowers?" Juanita asked. I thought I heard a hint of fear in her voice.

"Actually, you're much more dangerous than you think," Charles said. "Oh sure, your powers are worthless. But Grandpa has gone to great lengths to make sure that Baileys and Johnsons don't start talking to each other. That could ruin everything."

"Talking?" Juanita said. "You're afraid of a few kids talking?"

Charles's face turned dark. "You don't think talking can mess things up? We had a wonderful surprise planned for tonight. Right now every superhero in the city should have been in the stadium." His face became dark. "You see how many problems you've caused?"

He turned and walked back to the van.

"I'm starting to think we might be in big trouble," Benny said.

Charles climbed inside the vehicle and I noticed I dropped a little in the air. I wondered how much concentration it took to keep the three of us hovering.

The henchman returned. "Now I get to show you what happens when you go snooping around in the Jones family business." He pulled something from inside his coat pocket. At first I thought he had three long cigars taped together.

"Dynamite!" Benny said.

Charles flashed a wicked grin. "Grandpa likes it when I'm thorough. And of course, I like big bangs, so it's a win-win." He dropped the dynamite at our feet, patted his pockets, and pulled out a small box of matches. "It's my lucky day," he said. "I've only got one match left, but one match is all I need."

For a split second I had the wild idea that I would use my power to save the day. Charles had a match. I had a power that let me strike matches on polyester. Somehow everything would work out in the end.

But my power helped light matches. And more than anything on earth, I didn't want that match to burn.

My mind raced, but I couldn't think fast enough. Charles kneeled next to the pile, striking the match on the side of the box. His face glowed as the match flared.

I heard a noise off to my right, and the match went out.

"What the . . ." Charles said. "Why is my hand wet?" He looked up at Juanita. "Did you just spit at me?"

"I'm a Johnson." She shrugged. "I get a lot of practice."

Benny hooted.

Charles glared at Juanita and wiped his hand on his coat. His voice dripped with hate. "You silly girl. You think because now that I don't have a match, I'm going to let you all go free? All you've done is make it so I have to go get my lighter."

Charles shot Juanita one last menacing look, then turned and walked back to the van.

"What do we do?" Benny whispered.

Benny always looked to me for answers, but tonight I didn't have any. Not this time.

It felt like my world was crashing down around me. All I'd ever wanted was to save the day. And here we finally had a chance. Not just to fight the Johnsons, but to really save the day. To do something important. And when it really mattered, I'd come up short.

In the end, I didn't have what it took to be super.

"We can do this!" Benny said. "Rafter, you're the one who is always talking about tactics. What's our plan?"

I shook my head. "This is different, Benny. This is real."

Benny was pleading now. "Listen, pretend you're looking through the monitors. All of us are the green dots moving around. What would you tell us to do?"

I shook my head. "It's hopeless, Benny."

"Please." His voice was a whisper. "Just try."

Benny didn't get it. There was nothing to do. All was lost.

All is lost.

The words triggered something deep in the back of my mind. A voice—rough and gravelly—whispered to me. I recognized it at once.

The voice of Grandpa.

When all is lost, and hope is nowhere to be found. At that moment, a superhero stands up, looks evil right in the eyes, and says, "Is that the best you can do?"

I felt a low burn of anger.

Maybe I did get a worthless power, but that didn't mean *I* was worthless.

Taking a deep breath, I closed my eyes and drew a map in my mind—the garbage piles, the van, the tower. I placed four dots on the map—me, Benny, Juanita, and Charles. The three of us were immobile.

There had to be something.

No weapons. No phones.

There *had* to be something.

Our powers. I had to examine all the options. I had no matches. Juanita had no toilet. Benny could do his push-ups, but that wasn't—no, not push-ups. Benny's power was his belly button. But that didn't help either because—

Push-ups.

I opened my eyes. A single idea. I looked at Benny, judging the distance between the two of us. He nodded, and I saw complete trust in his face.

Charles was still rummaging around in the front of the van.

"Benny," I whispered. "Give me your hand!"

"What?" Benny asked. "I don't feel like holding hands right now."

"No, I need to be closer to you—grab my hand."

Benny reached out. I leaned as far as I could. We were still too far apart.

"Stretch," I said.

He reached out, his fingers quivering. Our hands were still a good six inches apart.

Juanita twisted in the darkness. "I think I can help." She bent at her waist and then reared back, kicking Benny in the backside. She drifted back, and Benny drifted forward.

"I never pass up a chance to kick a Bailey," Juanita said with a smile.

I reached out. "Gotcha!" I said, and pulled him close. I used Benny to spin myself in the air. I now faced Charles, who had just closed the door of the van. Benny was behind me.

"Okay," I whispered. "When I give the word, push me hard—right at Charles."

"What are you talking about?" Benny asked.

"You're the one who's been doing all those push-ups," I said. "Now is the time to see just how strong you are.

Remember, push me when I give you the word."

"What's the word?" Benny asked.

"Shhhh!" I hissed back.

Charles returned, a lighter in his hand. His smirk was maddening. He bent over and picked up the dynamite. "I hope you don't take this personally." He flicked the lighter. "I'm just following orders."

It took all of my concentration and control to keep my voice steady. "Hey, Chuck."

He looked up and sneered. I don't think he liked the nickname *Chuck*. "Yes? You want to beg for your life?"

I took a deep breath. "Is this the best you can do?"

"What?" Charles said, and I heard genuine confusion in his voice.

"I said, is this the best you can do? Because if it is, it's not enough to stop three superheroes."

Charles snorted. "You've got guts, kid," he said. "Too bad you're on the wrong side."

The lighter flared to life.

"*Now!*" I shouted, hoping beyond hope that Benny would understand that *now* was "the word."

He did.

Benny pushed me and I promised myself right then and there that I would never make fun of him for doing push-ups again. Because when he pushed me, he pushed me *hard*. I went flying toward Charles. The villain looked up, his eyes wide as he tried to move out of the way.

He was too late. I grabbed his trench coat and smashed against his left shoulder. We both went tumbling to the ground. The dynamite went flying, and I felt my stomach drop. The three sticks had a single wick extending from one end.

Sparks flew from the tip of the wick.

Charles ended up facedown in the snow, but he was already struggling to get up. I crawled forward, grabbing him in a headlock and trying to keep him immobile. I saw Benny and Juanita fall to the ground. Charles could only concentrate on so many things at once, and right now he must have been focused on me—or maybe the spitting wick just a few feet from our faces.

"Benny," I shouted. "Get the dynamite!" I kicked at one of Charles's legs as he tried to stand. He struggled against my grip, but I held him tight. He jammed an elbow in my ribcage, and I felt the breath go out of me.

I grabbed at his head and my hand came away with his stocking cap. I saw metal flashing in the moonlight.

"What the . . ." I couldn't help my surprise. Charles's head was shaved. Half of it was skin. The other half . . . a metallic dome. The dome was flush with the skin, almost as if his skull was made of metal, and part of the skin had come off.

I didn't exactly have time to ask him why half of his

head was a metal plate.

Juanita called from my right. "No one calls me silly." She dove at Charles's feet and wrapped her arms around his legs. He kicked with his heavy boots, but Juanita hung on for dear life. It reminded me of a cowboy riding a bull.

"Get off of me, you rotten kids."

Benny had the dynamite in his hand. It made me sick to see my brother holding explosives. No supersuit. Nothing to protect him.

"What do I do with it?" he yelled.

I doubted Benny could throw it far enough to keep us all safe, and I didn't know what would happen if he tried to pull the wick out.

I said the first thing that popped into my head.

"Put it in the glove compartment! It's a T9!"

Benny's face brightened. "Holy cow, you're right!" He raced toward the van, the wick bouncing and sparkling in the darkness.

Charles elbowed me in the teeth. I heard the van door open and close. Juanita let go of Charles and crawled away from the fight, leaving Charles to struggle to his feet.

"Juanita," I said. "Help." Juanita was kneeling in the mud, hunched over with her back toward me. She didn't turn around.

Benny came running, but he didn't get to us in time. Charles twisted and broke free of my grasp. I went sprawling into the dirt and before I could get up, the familiar disorientation filled my mind. For the second time that night, I found myself hovering in the cold air. Juanita and Benny were also trapped, spinning and floating six inches above the ground.

Charles got to his feet, seething and scowling. "You kids are really starting to get on my nerves," he said, his voice sounding like a growl. He wiped a trickle of blood from his nose, then picked up his stocking cap and placed it over his half-metal, half-skin head. "When I get finished with you—"

A crash broke the silence of the cold March night. It wasn't an explosion of three sticks of dynamite. It was more like .3 sticks of dynamite. The T9 had done its job.

Still, even .3 sticks of dynamite does damage. The explosion shattered the van windows, and flames poured upward toward the stars, silhouetting Charles against the yellow glow. The villain covered his head, and I watched as the passenger door of the van blew off its hinges. The vehicle lurched three feet into the air, then crashed back down to the ground. Smoke poured out of the windows, but the van still looked like it might be functional.

"Whoooo wheeee!" Benny shouted. "That T9 is one strong glove compartment."

Charles looked in disbelief at his smoking vehicle. "My van!" he said, then slowly turned to face the three of us. "You don't think I can do things the hard way?" His voice was cold. "You're about to find out just how unpleasant the hard way is." He leaned over and pulled a wicked-looking knife from one of his boots.

"Hey, Charles," Juanita said behind me. Her voice was surprisingly calm. "What does this button do?"

Charles looked confused for a split second, then he leaped forward.

Juanita held Charles's phone in her hand. The tower began to whine and crackle. Charles grabbed at the phone but Juanita was still floating. She kicked at his chest and held the phone out of his reach.

The noise grew until the tower seemed to scream with an electronic buzz. Then there was a flash of light and loud explosion.

The three of us went crashing to the ground.

22

DO YOU FEEL IT?

I pushed myself off the ground and felt a familiar tingling. The same tingling I'd felt just a few days ago, sitting on the piano bench.

Energy surged through the muscles of my arms, legs, and chest. Charles had his eyes closed and was breathing fast. Juanita was on her hands and knees, her head down. Benny was curled up in a ball.

Deep down, even before the sensation was complete, I knew what was happening.

I forced myself to stand. The tingling ran through my body. My bones buzzed, from my heels to my skull. Pressure built up inside my head. And then—exactly as it had on leap day—something clicked deep inside my brain.

My mind blossomed with understanding and knowledge. A final wave of energy rushed through me.

And then it was over.

Finally, after all this time, I had it.

My real power. My true power.

Juanita sat crouched on her feet. She steadied herself with one hand on the icy ground, and she held her other hand in front of her face, as if examining it.

Benny got to his feet—shock and delight covered his face. "Do you feel it, Rafter?"

I heard a rush of air, and Benny disappeared. I heard him whooping next to the van. Another whoosh of air, and he stood next to me once more.

"Speed!" he said, a giant grin covering his face. "I got speed!"

Charles had recovered. He jumped toward Juanita. "Give me my phone!"

Juanita didn't move, but Charles never touched her. I grabbed his wrist and held it firm. Tight enough that Charles would know my power, but not so tight as to crush any bones.

Strength.

Just like Grandpa.

I could slam my fist onto the ground and cause the earth to shake. I could walk to the van, shove my hands into the engine, and lift the vehicle up like an empty cardboard box. If I jumped, I would soar fifty feet into the air. And when I landed again, my muscles—my very bones—would withstand the impact.

Power surged through me—power that wanted to break free, and yet I had complete control.

I grabbed Charles by his arms. I lifted him in the air, then brought him down to me until our noses were almost touching. "This power is mine," I said. "And nobody will take it away from me again. Do you understand?"

"Please don't hurt me," Charles said. His voice sounded small.

"We're not going to hurt you," I said. "We're super-heroes. Although if you use your power on us again, we might make things a little uncomfortable for you."

Charles nodded. He didn't look too happy.

I couldn't help but smile. "Benny? Get the duct tape."

"I never leave home without it," Benny said. He dashed to the van and returned in a few seconds with his backpack. It was scorched, but the contents inside were in good shape. He ripped off a strip of tape and stepped toward the villain. "Now, Charles," Benny said, in his best tough-guy voice. "Do you want me to do this the easy way, or the hard way?"

Charles tried to run, but before he could take two steps, my brother had caught him and taped up his arms, hands, and legs. Benny finished with a strip of tape across his mouth. "I'm tired of hearing you talk." Benny stood over the villain, resting one leg on his chest, and then raising his arms in the air. "Somebody take a picture!" he yelled, and then with another whoop, he was gone, dashing around the dump.

I couldn't believe it. Just like that. We'd gotten our powers and beaten the villain.

We'd done the impossible.

I bent over Charles, who didn't look too happy about being taped up, and retrieved our phones. Juanita was standing now, holding her hands out in front of her. I held out her phone and she took it, dropping it into her pocket.

"Juanita?" I asked. "Are you okay?"

Juanita nodded absently. "Yeah. I'm okay." I could see tears in her eyes.

I wasn't sure what to say. What do you do when somebody says she is okay, but she doesn't appear to be okay?

"Did you not get the power you wanted?" I finally asked.

Juanita made a sound that sounded like a sob and a laugh, both trying to get out of her at once. "I'm sorry. I just wasn't ready for it."

"Ready for your power?"

Juanita nodded. "I got the same power as . . ." She lowered her head for just a moment, and then looked at me again. "I got the same power as my mom. And it makes me miss her."

Juanita looked so strong and so vulnerable, all at the same time. I wanted to put my arm around her, but I didn't dare.

"It's okay," she said. "I'm okay." She wrapped her arms around herself. "You know . . . with Mom gone, it's always just been me and Dad. He's great. He does so much for me but I've always felt like . . . I've always felt alone. But tonight, working with you and Benny . . ." Juanita looked at me. I felt like I should say something, but I didn't know what.

"Anyway," she said. "Thanks."

I cleared my throat. "What's your power?" I asked.

She smiled and pointed her hand at Charles. A rope of flame poured out of her hand and lit up the night sky. It arced across the darkness, passing a foot over Charles, who was lying on the ground. He tried to scream in terror, but the duct tape kept him relatively quiet.

"Whoa," said Benny, who had materialized in a rush of wind. "That is some wild stuff."

Juanita smiled. "This is how they did it," she said, holding up Charles's phone. "This controls the tower. This gives or takes away powers."

"Does that mean everybody has their power back?" I asked. I tried to imagine my entire extended family with Juanita's entire family, all with their powers back.

That could be ugly.

Juanita tossed me the phone. "I think so. There are only two settings. Real powers or fake powers."

I looked at the phone. It was a simple interface. I selected the tower menu, and two buttons appeared on the screen. The red button took away powers. The green button gave them back.

I had an idea.

I slipped Charles's phone into my pocket, and pulled out my other phone. "Juanita," I said. "Call your family. Tell them to come here."

"Why?" Juanita asked.

I pulled up Dad's number on the screen. "We need to do what Oscar Redding could never do. We need to get both families together, right now. We need to start talking, and we need to prove once and for all who the real villains are. If that doesn't get the families to stop fighting, nothing will."

Juanita nodded, and pulled out her phone.

We'd done it. Three kids without real powers had done the impossible—we'd saved the day.

That is when the black helicopter descended from the sky.

23

WOULD YOU BE SO KIND AS TO EXPLAIN THIS MESS?

In a flash, Benny was by my side. "What's that sound?" he asked.

I had just spotted the aircraft and pointed toward the flashing lights in the sky. "Helicopter. It must be Dirk."

"I don't think that's one of ours," Benny said.

He was right. It didn't have the Bailey family colors. I looked over at Juanita. "You guys have helicopters?"

She shook her head. "If we have one, I've never seen it."

The helicopter came to a rest on the ground. I could see the moon and stars reflected on the gleaming black metal.

Wind from the blades tore at my coat, and I took an involuntary step back, shielding my eyes. The engine began to wind down. For a moment nothing happened. The helicopter sat there like a bug staring at us, as if it was waiting for us to make the first move.

There was no question in my mind.

The Jones family had arrived.

The tactical side of my brain took over. Inside the helicopter were Joneses, but I had no idea how many or what powers they had. What I did know was that there were only three of us to stand against them. I still had my phone in my hand, and it still had Dad's number on the screen. I hit the send button.

"Hello?" I heard Dad's voice. I also heard a lot of shouting. "Rafter, I'm a bit busy. One of the Johnsons has Uncle Ralph in a headlock, and your Aunt Verna won't stop—"

I saw Juanita pull out her own phone.

"Dad," I said. "You have to get to the city dump. Benny and I are here. Dad, there are supervillains."

"What are you talking about?" Dad said. "We saw that strange light again and we all got our powers back. We're fighting the entire Johnson clan right—"

"Dad," I said. "There's no time to explain. Benny and I are in trouble."

That was all it took.

"Trouble?" I heard Dad cover the phone with his hand, then heard a muffled shout through the phone. "It's the boys. They're in danger!" Dad's voice became louder on the phone. "We'll be there in ten minutes."

Juanita spoke into her phone. After a moment, she hung up and said, "My family's on the way too."

I looked at the helicopter. The whine of the motor became quieter, and the blades slowed.

We had to stall for ten minutes.

We had to *survive* for ten minutes.

At least we had our powers.

The helicopter door slid open. A pilot sat at the controls. In the middle section of the helicopter, where three or even four people could have fit, sat a single man—a man who took up the entire space.

I've never seen anybody as big as the man who stepped out of the helicopter. He had to bend over at the waist until he was out from under the blades. He wore a suit—not a supersuit, but an actual suit and tie. The man was bald, just like Charles, and I was surprised to see a similar metal plate attached to his head. He had a round and puffy face, and his eyes were thin, black slits. When he stood up straight, I realized he had to be at least seven feet tall.

He had arms like tree branches and legs as thick as telephone poles. The man looked strong. Terribly strong.

I smiled in the darkness. *My first real challenge.*

The man's head was like a rock. It turned first one way, and then the other. His gaze rested on Charles, who was still lying on the ground. He'd somehow managed to get his hands in front of him and had pulled the tape from his mouth.

The giant spoke, his voice deep and rough. "Charles, would you be so kind as to explain this mess?"

Charles struggled to sit up. "There's no mess, Grandpa. I had . . . uh . . . a minor setback, that's all. I was just about to wrap things up when you got here."

Grandpa. The large man standing before me was the head of the entire family—October Jones.

The giant paused for a moment, not saying a word. The silence was awkward. Finally, he spoke again. "Well then, Charles. If you've got everything under control, I'll see you back at headquarters."

"No!" Charles said, getting up on his knees. "Grandpa, I'm sorry. I . . . these kids, they . . . they're monsters! Please, Grandpa, I need your help."

The big guy turned to look at Benny, Juanita, and me. Another pause.

The tactics side of my brain tingled. Something wasn't right.

"So you've been beaten by three children?" the giant said. "Charles, just when I think you can't set my expectations any lower, you botch things up in ways I couldn't possibly believe." The giant laughed, and it sounded like a cement truck barreling down a gravel road.

My heart pounded, but I cleared my mind. I looked around, drawing the dump again in my head. Each person and vehicle became a dot. Charles, Juanita, Benny, the giant, the helicopter, the van. I made a list of anything I had to use in a fight. Something still tickled the back of my mind.

"Enough!" the giant roared. "Charles, it's time you learn a lesson. Watch how it's done."

The giant began to walk toward us. I was probably imagining it, but I thought I felt the ground shaking under our feet.

I looked at the helicopter. At the giant. He kept pausing before he spoke. What was I missing?

I saw a flash of light on the side of the giant's head. Moonlight reflected in the darkness.

And I knew the answer.

I formed a plan. "Benny," I said, speaking slow and clear. "When I give the word, you go left. Make sure Charles doesn't interfere. If he tries to levitate anybody, keep him busy."

Benny nodded, a fierce smile creeping over his face.

"Juanita," I said. "You go right and try to distract the giant."

"Wait a minute," Juanita said. "You want me to take on . . . the big guy? Aren't you the one who just got super-strength?"

The giant was twenty feet from us. "Use your power." I pointed to the van. "Or if the van still works, see if you can distract him with that."

Juanita looked like she wanted to argue, but there was no point in waiting any longer. "Go!" I shouted.

Both of them moved—our first battle, and still we were working like a team. Benny went left, Juanita right. I stepped forward, walking toward the giant.

We met in the middle and stopped. I had to look up to see his face. His head turned, first to look at Benny, then at Juanita. Finally, his gaze came to rest on me.

I felt power surging through my muscles. The man before me was strong. He had to be. But I was stronger.

Again, the pause. The giant stood there, as if he didn't know what to say—or what to do. And then he spoke. "Tonight is not your lucky night, little boy."

"No," I said. "I believe it is."

Two things happened at once. To my left, Charles got to his feet, only to be rewarded by Benny charging into his stomach. They both fell to the ground.

To my right, the black and smoldering van roared to life. Juanita sat behind the wheel, tugging at the gear shift. The wipers turned on, then off. The van lurched, stopped, and then lurched again. The giant turned his head to look at the van. The headlights flared to life, and the giant shielded his eyes. With the van lights bathing us, I could see it—a small coil of wire coming out of the collar of the suit, ending in the giant's ear.

An earpiece.

October Jones—the real villain—was here, but he wasn't the hulking figure in front of me. Every time the giant had spoken, there had been a pause—as if he'd been waiting for instructions. I remembered a line from *The Wizard of Oz*—"Pay no attention to that man behind the curtain."

I raced forward. Not at the hulking figure, but around him. Toward the helicopter.

Sitting in the pilot's seat was a figure—a small figure, bent over and frail—almost invisible behind the windshield. If my hunch was right, this was the real October Jones.

24

MY NAME IS RAFTER

I ran. The helicopter door stood open, but I guess it didn't matter. With my new power I could have ripped the door off its hinges. I could have torn a hole in the side of the aircraft. The pilot made no move to close the door. He wasn't worried about me.

In the back of my mind, a warning bell went off.

I couldn't turn around now. To my right the van lurched forward. Juanita extended her hand out of the window, shooting fire from her palm. To my left, Benny was tickling a furious Charles.

Inside the helicopter—silence.

I reached the door and climbed inside.

And came face to face with October Jones.

The first thing I noticed was that the supervillain wore a simple flight suit—not a supersuit. My mind raced; I felt almost frantic. This man didn't have a supersuit. Leader of the whole Jones family and he didn't feel the need to put on protection or dress up in a costume.

He wore a helmet, and his face was partially hidden by a stretch of black fabric that went from the bottom of his left jaw, over his mouth and nose, and attached to the helmet above his right ear.

Gray hair poked out from under the helmet, and wrinkles covered his face, but I couldn't guess at his age. He might have been forty, or sixty, or eighty.

The man had cold eyes, and yet at the same time they seethed with fire. If he felt fear, his face revealed none of it. The man sitting in the pilot's chair was in complete control.

That scared me more than anything.

"Get out of my helicopter, boy," the man said. "Now."

His calm voice unnerved me. With great effort, I kept my own words steady, trying to match his. "I'm not a boy. My name is Rafter. Rafter Bailey. And your name is October Jones."

I'd guessed right. Fury grew in October's face. He twisted toward me in his seat, and shouted angrily, "I don't care what your name is or who you are. I told you to get out of my helicopter!"

I didn't move.

With lightning speed, he jumped out of his seat, pushing my shoulders. I could've stopped him. With my strength, no one would push me around ever again. But I let him think he had the upper hand, and I fell out of the helicopter and landed on the ground. October lifted his wrist to his mouth and said something I couldn't hear.

I stood, shaking myself off. The reflection of the window let me see the hulking figure turn and pound his way toward us. October still crouched by the door of the helicopter. I reached inside and grabbed the villain by his flight suit.

But before I could pull, October grabbed my wrist. He pierced me with a cold stare. "I do not have time for this, little boy. I'll deal with you myself, if I must."

One second he was in the helicopter, hand gripping my wrist. The next second he pushed me back, and both of us stood on the ground. He grabbed the front of my coat in a death grip. I did not like the look in his eyes.

And then, very suddenly, we were soaring into the cold night sky. Wind roared past my ears. I felt my stomach drop.

The lights of the city beneath my feet became little more than tiny points. I didn't know how high we were—a thousand, maybe fifteen hundred feet—and still we shot toward the stars. I didn't like my chances of surviving a fall at this height, even with my new superpower.

Tactics. Another piece of information. October's power

was flight. I still had a slight advantage with my strength.

The air rushing past my ears grew quiet as we slowed and came to a stop. We hovered in the sky, surrounded by inky darkness. October had me at arm's length, like you might carry a leaking bag of garbage. I reached out and grabbed the front of his flight suit. If he let go of me, I wouldn't fall.

"I grow tired of this, boy." October's voice sounded quiet in the stillness of the sky.

"I told you," I said, trying to make my voice as calm as his. It was even harder because my teeth were chattering in the cold. "My name is Rafter."

"And I told you . . ." October paused. His face broke into a sneer. "Wait a minute. You're one of the new ones, right?" His laugh was as cold as the March night air.

Hanging on to October's suit wasn't secure enough for me. I swung forward, wrapping my legs around his waist.

"Oh, this is delicious," October said. "Let me get this straight. I give you a worthless power, and somehow you still manage to track me down?"

I'd heard the word *worthless* one too many times. I pulled October close and wrapped my arms around him until I had him in a full-body bear hug. I curled my legs together, squeezing his waist in an iron grip, and doing the same with my arms—not hard enough to break anything, but enough to constrict his breathing. I wanted him to know who he was dealing with. Not some worthless kid, but a superhero.

October merely laughed.

"Afraid of heights?" He mocked.

I squeezed harder. This much pressure would crush the ribs of a normal person, but it seemed to be having no effect on October. Maybe his flight suit had armor after all. Or maybe . . .

No.

I squeezed with all my might. I grunted with effort. October showed no pain. The only way he could survive my grip was if . . . he had superstrength, too.

October Jones was a Super-super.

25

DO YOU SEE THAT?

I knew real fear in that moment. October could shock me with electricity. He could burn me with fire or lava. That's why he acted like he was in total control . . . because he *was*.

Looking down, I desperately hoped that he'd somehow lost focus and drifted downward. That my muscles and bones could withstand a fall. If I could pry myself away from him, maybe I'd have a chance.

Too high. We were still too high.

My mind raced, but I could think of nothing. October had me right where he wanted me. He could finish the job at any time.

Staring at the ground below us, I noticed something

looked out of place. At first I couldn't figure out what, and then I saw it.

Up here, the entire city was a grid. On that grid were little points of light, just like on the battle maps I always used to form strategies. Some lights didn't move—those must have been street lamps and house lights. Other lights—probably cars or trucks—crept slowly along the dark lines of streets.

At first glance, it was little more than chaos, with lights moving every which way. But if you looked at it . . . if you really looked, you could see the pattern.

There. And there. And there. Dozens of cars—maybe as many as thirty—all moving from a single place and headed in the same direction.

Moving from First Dam, toward the city dump.

The Baileys and the Johnsons—true superheroes—were on their way to save the day.

"Do you see that?" I asked.

October looked down. "I see nothing but a very long drop."

The fear hadn't left me, but knowing that my family was on their way gave me courage.

"The Baileys," I said. "And the Johnsons. Superheroes. All of them. Coming to save us." I looked back up at October. "Coming to fight you."

He looked down. I thought I saw just a flicker of

surprise, but then it was gone.

"Superheroes?" The amusement was back in his voice. "They are buffoons."

October threw back his head and laughed. It was an ugly laugh, and the darkness amplified it.

"I think I like you after all," October said. "I had a plan to execute tonight, and you got in the way. But here you've gone and gathered all the Baileys and the Johnsons to one place, just like I wanted. That makes it ever so convenient for me. This must be your way of asking for forgiveness."

Looking back down at the city, I felt a tightness in my chest. My family—and Juanita's—was walking into a trap.

I hadn't saved the day. I'd ruined it.

My mind raced. There had to be something I could do. This time, all of our lives depended on it. But what could I do against a super-super? I had my power—I finally had my strength—but it wasn't enough. My power didn't make me super. I needed something more.

It's not your power that makes you super. It's what you do with that power.

What you do with that power.

I knew there was only one thing to do.

26

I HAVE A QUESTION FOR YOU, MR. JONES

Simple tactics in theory, but not so simple to do. Not after everything I'd been through.

If your opponent outguns you, you take away his guns.

I reached into my pocket for the phone. Charles's phone.

It was still on the same screen as when I'd slipped it in my pocket. Two buttons glowed in the darkness—one of them green, the other red.

"I have a question for you, Mr. Jones," I said.

"And I think I'm done with you, boy." October's eyes looked like an angry gray sea. "It's time to sweep up this little mess, and deposit it in the dump where it belongs."

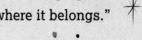

I held up the phone so that October could see it. "How long do we have until the tower goes off?"

I pressed the red button, and dropped the phone.

Below us, a high-pitched noise got louder and louder. The white sphere at the top of the tower began to crackle with energy.

A series of emotions crossed October's face—confusion, understanding, fury.

And finally . . . fear.

October Jones was no longer in control.

27

DON'T THINK THIS IS OVER

I leaned forward and held tight to October. He could still use his powers to hurt me, but anything he did would take time. And if the tower went off—all the way up here—he and I would fall. He only had a split second to act, and I was betting he would think of his own safety first.

He did.

For the second time that night, October and I raced through the night. October flew toward the earth at a gut-wrenching speed. In a matter of seconds the dump went from being a small circle I could cover with my hand to the only thing in my vision. October slowed as we neared the ground. I pushed off and fell the last forty feet. My heels slammed into the ground, cutting

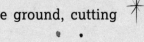

powerful furrows as I came to a halt. Mud and snow showered into the air. I fell forward, my muscles straining against the force of gravity. I rolled to my side with no broken bones.

The tower went off. A flash of light lit up the dump. Thunder crashed and the noise echoed off garbage heaps.

This time I knew what to expect—it felt like somebody flicking a switch. One moment I had my power, and the next moment it was gone. Replaced with the weaker one. If I had a match and could find a beat-up couch or leisure suit in the dump, I could once again provide fire.

The flash of the light had ruined my night vision, and it took a minute for my eyes to readjust to the darkness. I got to my knees and took in everything around me. Charles sprinted toward the helicopter. Somehow he'd freed himself from the tape. The giant also moved toward the helicopter. The van lay on its side, and Juanita crawled up through the driver's-side window.

October stepped toward me, shaking with rage. I scanned the ground, looking for the phone. I saw shards of plastic and broken circuits a few feet away. Of course the phone wouldn't survive the fall.

I fell backward, watching in fear as October approached.

But then Benny was there, pulling me to my feet. And Juanita hustled over, fierce and unafraid. I stood, and the three of us faced the villain.

October seethed. "You spent all this time trying to get your power, and when you finally have it, you throw it away?"

I stared at him, not knowing what to say.

October spit out his words. "You're a fool."

"No," Benny said. "He's a superhero."

I could see the hatred in October's face, but it was a calculating hatred. Hatred that could wait to get revenge. As far as he was concerned, October Jones was once again in control.

"Don't think this is over," he said. "Now I know your name, Rafter Bailey, and believe me, that's not a good thing." Shooting one last glance at the three of us, he turned and strode to his helicopter.

Benny stepped forward, but I grabbed his coat and held him back.

"We can stop him," Benny said. "He's nothing but an old geezer now. He has no powers."

I shook my head. "He's anything but an old geezer," I said. "Plus, he still has that giant on his side. And who knows what kind of weapons he might have in the helicopter. Let's not push our luck."

October got in the helicopter and sat behind the controls. The engines whined, and a moment later the aircraft lifted a dozen feet into the sky.

The helicopter slowly turned until it was pointing at the tower.

A single missile streaked across the dump, slamming into the side of the RV. It burst into flames and the fire licked the wooden tower. In another minute, the tower leaned and then crashed to the ground. The white sphere burned.

Silence settled over the dump. My legs felt like rubber. I sank to the ground. The solid earth felt good.

Benny stared into the sky. I couldn't read his expression. Juanita watched the tower burn, her face flickering orange and red.

I'd lost my real power. And with the tower destroyed, I had no idea how to get it back. But in that moment—sitting in the dump with my brother and my friend—I didn't care. Oh, I still wanted my power. Somehow I'd figure out how to fix everything. But for now it didn't matter. Because right then, for the first time in my life, I felt almost super.

28

YOU CAN'T JUST IGNORE THE LAWS OF MATHEMATICS

One by one family members arrived. One by one they got out of their cars and, without even a beat's hesitation, started yelling at members of the other family. Adults standing there in their supersuits, shaking fists and spitting. There was even the occasional headlock and chest poke.

Juanita, Benny, and I just stood there.

Dad, who had apparently been caught in a yelling match with a Johnson, finally spotted Benny and me and seemed to remember why he was there. He threw his hands up into the air, spun on his heels, and walked over toward us.

"I thought you said you were in trouble. We all lost our powers again on the way over—Ah!" he pointed at Juanita. "I see you've captured a Johnson. Is she the trouble?" He shook his fist.

Juanita's dad was standing close. "You think three Baileys are enough to capture my daughter?" Mr. Johnson turned his head and spit. "I hate to tell you this, but she has you outnumbered."

"How could we be outnumbered?" Dad asked. "There are three of us, and one of her. You can't just ignore the laws of mathematics."

I rolled my eyes. "Dad, this is Juanita Johnson. She helped us."

"She helped you? You mean with *this*?" Dad motioned at the burning tower. "Yeah, that sounds about right. Anytime a Johnson *helps out*"—Dad made air quotes with his fingers—"this is usually how it ends up. Although I have to admit, that's a really nice fire."

Juanita's dad stepped forward with his finger raised. I could tell he was going to engage in some chest poking.

"Dad!" I shouted. "Mr. Johnson! I have something to tell both of you, and I want you to listen without interrupting."

Dad looked like he might protest, then folded his arms and waited. Mr. Johnson turned his back on me, but he didn't walk away.

While the rest of our families yelled and wrestled

around us, I told both of the adults everything I knew about the Joneses. About how Grandpa Jones was keeping our families fighting so that he could do whatever he wanted without interference from superheroes. I explained about the tower, and the powers, and how we'd finally beaten October Jones—at least for now.

By the time I'd finished, Mr. Johnson had turned around, and I noticed Uncle Ralph, Jessie, and my new algebra teacher, Juanita's uncle, were all standing close, listening.

"I missed half of the story," the Johnsons said. "Back up and start from the beginning."

This time Juanita told it. By the time she was done, half of the family members were listening, and the other half were realizing that no one was fighting anymore. Finally, Benny told the whole story a third time. He made sure that everybody knew it was his push-ups that made the entire thing possible.

When Benny finished, everyone looked stunned.

Dad was the first one to speak. "The thing I don't get is why only you new heroes lost your powers in the beginning? Why didn't we all lose our powers?"

I had wondered the same thing. "All I can figure is that maybe they hadn't perfected their technology. Maybe Benny, Juanita, and I were the guinea pigs. Once they saw that it worked, they built the larger tower and took away everybody's powers at once."

Dad frowned, but nodded. "I guess we won't know for sure unless we track one of them down."

No one said anything for several moments. I took a deep breath. This was the hard part. "We all have worthless powers now," I said. "And we're up against an entire family of supervillains who could either have another device to give them their powers back, or at the very least, know how to make one." I paused and let that sink in. "Within a few hours, or maybe a few days or weeks, there will be supervillains with powers right here in the city."

"We have to stop the fighting and work together," Juanita said.

"I don't help Baileys," a Johnson said, spitting onto the snow.

"We don't have time for you people to be thick-headed," Juanita said. I looked down to hide my smile. I was starting to appreciate the way Juanita didn't pull any punches.

I found Grandpa in the crowd of Baileys. "Grandpa," I said. "You are the senior Bailey here. Will you agree to stop fighting the Johnsons? At least until we can find out what is going on?"

Grandpa looked thoughtful. "I've sworn to fight evil," he said. "I can't just—"

I turned to Juanita's grandmother, who had come to stand by her granddaughter. "Mrs. Johnson," I said. "My grandpa thinks you're a supervillain. Do you and the rest of your family promise, starting right now, to stop your evil ways?"

I wish I could have captured the look on Grandmother Johnson's face. Her eyes grew wide and her mouth opened and closed for at least three seconds before she could speak. "We are not, nor have we ever been . . ."

I'd only known Juanita for about a week now, and already she understood how I thought. "Rafter's not saying we're supervillains, Grandmother. He's asking you if any of us intend to do anything evil in the near future."

"Of course not!" Grandmother Johnson said. "I can speak for every Johnson here when I say—"

I jumped in. "Grandpa, Mrs. Johnson just promised that their family will stop being evil. Will you agree not to fight them anymore?"

"But she's a supervillain!" Dad said. "She's probably lying!"

"Now, son," Grandpa said. "This boy's talking some sense. Family huddle."

Grandpa put his arm around Dad's shoulder. A few other Baileys stepped forward and spoke in low voices.

Grandpa folded his arms and stepped forward. "I don't know if a Johnson can really reform." He unfolded his arms to shake his fist, then folded them again. "But as a superhero, I believe in mercy and justice. We won't battle any of you villains until we hear of you—"

"Not hear," I said. "The Joneses will just call us up pretending to be citizens and we'll be fighting again tomorrow morning. You have to actually see them doing something wrong."

Grandpa folded his arms and blew air through his mustache. "Okay. Until we *see* them doing something worth battling against."

"Done!" I shouted. "Mrs. Johnson, will you agree to the same thing? If my family promises not to do any more evil, will you promise not to fight us?"

Grandmother Johnson stared at Grandpa, her fingernails tapping her glass cane.

"I must point out," Dad said, raising a finger, "that our family has never done any evil in the first place."

Grandmother Johnson continued to tap her fingernails, and then turned to Grandpa. "I don't know if it was a Jones or a Bailey that stole our powers." She paused long enough to spit. "But I know evil when I see it. If there really is a new family in town, then my granddaughter is right. We must put aside our differences and focus our energies."

For a moment, no one said anything. I felt like I was trying to catch a bubble without breaking it.

"I'll be watching you, Mrs. Johnson," Grandpa finally said.

"And I, you, Mr. Bailey," Grandmother Johnson replied.

With that, she turned and walked toward one of the cars. In a moment, both Baileys and Johnsons had separated and were talking among themselves.

Dad came over and put his arms around me and Benny. "I'm proud of you boys. Let's get you home and you can tell me all about your first battle. I'm sorry I missed it."

"We'll be there in a second, Dad." I said. He raised an eyebrow, and I looked over at Juanita, who was talking to her dad.

"Ah. Yes." Dad went and stood by his car.

Juanita left her dad and came over to stand by me and Benny. For a moment, none of us said anything. Then Benny started grinning, and the next thing I knew we were all laughing.

"We did it, didn't we?" I said. "I mean we really did it."

"Maybe," Juanita said. "How long do you think the truce will last?" I could hear doubt in her voice.

"I bet Aunt Verna has already tried to pull over one of your relatives for speeding," Benny said.

"I don't know," I said. "I think it will last. Did you see what happened? There at the end?"

Juanita looked at me, confused. She shook her head.

"Both of them said the other person's name," I said.

Juanita got it. "Grandma didn't spit."

"And Grandpa didn't shake his fist," Benny replied.

I nodded. "Maybe this truce will stick after all."

Benny started jogging in place. "We have *got* to get our real powers back. That was SO COOL! What are we going to do next?"

I shrugged. "We put our bikes in the trunk and go home."

"No," Benny said. "After that. How are we going to track down October Jones?"

Juanita looked at me, waiting for an answer.

There was so much to do, and I didn't know where to start. I looked from Benny to Juanita, and then smiled.

"We'll wing it."

29

NO ONE ANSWERED

I crawled into bed that night exhausted. I was certain I'd fall asleep as soon as my head hit the pillow, but it didn't happen. Lying in the darkness, I felt like everywhere I looked I saw the face of October Jones.

Now I know your name, Rafter Bailey, and believe me, that's not a good thing.

I tried pushing the thoughts away. This was the best day of my life. I'd done what I'd always dreamed of. . . . I had saved the day.

The door to our room opened a crack. Light spilled in from the hall. Benny raised his head and the door opened all the way.

I could see Dad's silhouette in the light, but something

seemed wrong. His shoulders slouched. It looked like he was carrying a heavy weight on his back.

"Can I come in?" Dad asked.

"Sure," I sat up in bed. "What's up?"

Dad lowered himself to the edge of my bed. Benny slipped out from under his covers and came and sat next to him.

Dad ran his finger through his hair and didn't say anything for a while.

"Is everything okay?" I finally asked.

Dad smiled, but I noticed he didn't answer my question. "I want you boys to know how proud I am of you. I just got off the phone with Grandpa. It's hard to believe we've been deceived for this long. I mean . . . Grandpa can't even remember a time when we weren't fighting the Johnsons. And here you boys uncover the truth, and then find the real villain, and then stop him. . . ." His voice trailed off.

He did sound proud, but he also sounded tired. Dad was the kind of guy who would make a speech and clap you on the back at a moment like this.

"What's wrong?" Benny asked. He could sense it too.

Dad put his hand on my shoulder, and around Benny. "First, I want to apologize. It was wrong of your mother and me to decide that since you didn't get . . . real powers, that you couldn't be super. You've shown to the entire family that this isn't true. I'm sorry I doubted you."

"Does this mean we will finally get supersuits?" Benny asked.

Dad smiled. "It most certainly does. You boys have taught me that you don't need powers to be super. You are super every bit as much as any of us, and so you need your supersuits. You can help with the design, first thing in the morning."

I could feel Benny shaking on the bed, barely able to contain his excitement.

Dad cleared his throat. "I don't want you boys to be scared. Like I said, I just got off the phone with Grandpa. He's proud of you two boys as well. But he called my great-aunt Jewel over in Oak City. Just to report in."

"And?" Benny asked.

"No one answered the phone." Dad fell silent.

"Well, it's late," Benny said. "Maybe . . ."

Benny knew as well as I did that somebody was *always* by the phone.

Dad continued. "He called the Denver line. And New York. He called London, Moscow, Brisbane. He said he called at least twenty different lines." Dad sighed, rubbing his forehead. "No one answered. Anywhere."

I tried to slow my breathing. I could feel my heart thumping in my chest.

Dad continued. "We've been fighting the Johnsons all

over the world, wherever they happen to be. And now . . ."
Dad pushed his fingers through his hair. "Grandpa called
Mrs. Johnson. Juanita's grandmother. She tried calling
Johnsons in other cities. She tried calling them every-
where. She found the same thing. No one answered. No
one is out there."

"What does that mean?" I asked.

Dad shook his head. "I don't know for sure, but I can
guess. Whatever this Jones family was trying to do here
in Split Rock, they tried to do everywhere else. And from
the look of it, they succeeded."

Dad sat quiet for a moment, and then said, "We might
be the only superheroes left."

I couldn't imagine it. I didn't see a lot of my relatives in
other cities. They were distant cousins, uncles, and aunts.
People I didn't even know. But I'd always felt comfort in
the fact that they were out there, fighting the same fight
that I was. Standing up for goodness everywhere. And
now . . . all gone? It couldn't be true.

"We don't even have our real powers anymore."
Benny's voice sounded small in the darkness. "All the
superheroes are missing, and now there's a new family of
supervillains?"

"The superheroes in Split Rock still stand." Dad
straightened up. "Thanks to you two." He squeezed my
shoulder. "There are Baileys in this city, and there are

Johnsons in this city. If we work together—and we *are* going to work together—then we can still be strong. If the Joneses want this city, they will have to come through us."

We spoke a little bit longer—floating voices in the pale light from the hall. We talked about Joneses and Johnsons, about supersuits and the motor pool. We talked about being super and doing good.

Finally Dad stood. "It's time for you boys to get some sleep. We might have some dangerous days ahead of us."

Dad left the room. He turned off the light in the hall, making the darkness complete. I could hear Benny breathing in his bed, and in a short time his breaths were steady and deep.

I could feel sleep overtaking me. I closed my eyes. This time the face of October Jones didn't appear. This time I didn't hear his words.

I heard my father.

The superheroes in Split Rock still stand. If the Joneses want this city, they will have to come through us.

Turn the page for a sneak peek
at the **SUPER ACTION-PACKED** sequel!

1.

VERY FINE SCREAMING, SON

The only good thing about hanging like a sleeping baby—
strapped to your father's belly in an oversized canvas
carrier—is that he can't see it when you roll your eyes.

But let me back up.

Dad and I hovered over a lake. It was almost midnight
and the Milky Way spread across the sky like sparkling
morning mist.

"Uh . . ." Dad's voice came from behind me. My arms
and legs hung down in front of me like . . . well, like a sleeping baby's. "You don't by any chance know where we are,
do you, Rafter?"

That isn't what made me want to roll my eyes. Dad getting lost wasn't anything new.

Usually when Dad and I go flying, he picks me up and leaps into the air. I'm thirteen and not exactly a lightweight, but he has a supersuit that gives him extra strength. And flying is his superpower. Or rather, *was* his superpower.

Tonight, it wasn't his power that kept us hovering over the lake. It was a military-grade jetpack strapped to his back. He needed one hand to work the controls, and the other to hold his phone so he could use the map application.

That's why I was in the oversized canvas baby carrier.

"Sorry, Dad, I have no idea where we are," I replied. "I wasn't paying attention."

A cluster of lights poked through the darkness on the far side of the lake, but not enough to be the city of Three Forks, our destination. Actually, I didn't think Three Forks even had a lake.

"Well, drat," Dad said. "This map application seems to be broken. Also, everything is in French."

This still wasn't when I rolled my eyes.

My dad is amazing. He's a superhero. He's also the only person I know who can get lost carrying a GPS-enabled super-smartphone.

Dad put the phone in a pocket of his supersuit. I should have brought my phone but I didn't have any pockets. I still didn't have a supersuit of my own. I was wearing black sweatpants and a black long-sleeved shirt.

Dad punched the small screen on his supersuit. The

jetpack whined louder and we started moving.

I found the North Star off to the right, which meant we were heading west. That was at least the right general direction.

The breeze against my face carried a hint of warmth. Summer lurked around the corner, and the air up here was clear and fresh. I filled my lungs with the sweetness. It felt good to be outside. Really good. I'd spent too much time indoors the past few months, doing something my Dad called *hunkering down.*

I'd started hating those two words. Hunkering down. They were supposed to sound active. Like maybe we were hiding in the trenches, waiting for the right time to charge. But really they were just a fancy way of saying we were hiding. Hiding from supervillains.

One in particular—October Jones.

I stretched out my hands, feeling the breeze rush between my fingers like water in a stream. I loved to fly. Usually, my younger brother, Benny, and I fought over who got to go out flying with Dad. But two weeks ago Benny had downloaded a new game to his phone called Virtual Goat Ranch. Now he spent his extra time raising virtual goats. Apparently, three of his goats were pregnant, and he wanted to be there as soon as the baby goats were born so he could give them names.

Dad picked up speed and the wind grew to a roar. It

didn't matter how many times I flew, I never grew tired of it. Whatever problems I had in my life, at two thousand feet everything looked peaceful. Up in the empty sky. Alone.

"Try not to move around so much," Dad called out. "You're throwing off my balance."

Well, not exactly alone.

"Sorry, Dad!" I shouted over the noise.

We flew for another twenty minutes or so before Dad slowed down.

"Is that a swamp down there?" he asked. "Does Three Forks have swamps? I *told* your mother we should have waited until morning."

Dad looked to his right. "Wait a minute. Is that . . . is that Mount Rushmore?"

Right there. *That* is when I rolled my eyes. But like I said, from my spot in the big baby carrier, Dad couldn't see me.

"Not unless we've traveled eight hundred miles off course, Dad."

"That does it," Dad said. "I'm calling your mother. She's going to have to look us up on the tracking system and give us directions."

Dad started unzipping zippers and opening pockets on his suit.

I had a sickening thought. "Just don't unbuckle my—"

I heard the whip of canvas passing through a metal buckle, and then the snug material around my waist went slack. I fell, tumbling through the night sky.

Not again, I thought.

Stars and lights from the ground spun in dizzying circles. Wind rushed loud in my ears, but I could hear Dad's voice calling from somewhere above. "I told you not to wiggle!"

It wasn't my wiggling that had made me fall, but I decided that now wasn't the best time to start an argument.

"Um . . . ," I yelled (and yelling "um" is harder than it sounds). "Dad, can I get a little help here?"

I spread out my arms and legs so that I stopped spinning. I estimated I had at least twenty seconds before I hit the ground.

"I can't tell where you are!" Dad's voice sounded closer this time and to the right. "It might help if you scream."

I could hear teasing in Dad's voice, but just to be safe, I screamed. I screamed for a solid five seconds until I felt Dad's arms around me.

"There you are," Dad said. "Very fine screaming, son."

"I get a lot of practice." I rolled my eyes for the second time that night.

"Hey, look there." Dad pointed. "It's Three Forks!"

Sure enough, the familiar Three Forks Sugar Beet Factory loomed off to our left, its large cement smokestacks cutting into the sky.

Dad strapped me back into the carrier and then flew down to read a street sign. He flew up, over, and back down to read another. He repeated this until I felt certain the mashed potatoes and chard I'd eaten for dinner were having a wrestling match in my belly.

Finally, we reached our destination—an old house just beyond the city limits where we were supposed to meet my cousin.

Well, I use the word *cousin* loosely. I have hundreds of relatives—maybe a thousand. Uncles, aunts, cousins, second cousins, cousins once removed. We're spread out all over. There are Baileys in every major city and township in the country. I've found it's easiest just to call everybody cousin, unless they're old. Then they're an aunt or uncle. If they're really old, or look a little insecure, I call them great-aunt or great-uncle.

Dad landed on the lawn. Or what had been the lawn once. Now it was mostly weeds, dead grass, and crusty dirt. Paint peeled from the small white clapboard house. Brown vines clung to the walls, as if they were trying to pull the building into the earth. Bits of trash lay scattered around the yard.

I checked the address on the side of the home. "Who are

we meeting here again?"

"John Bailey," Dad said. "And his nephew. They were the only survivors of the Joneses' attack here in Three Forks."

He took off the jetpack and leaned it against the porch. Dad climbed the stairs, then rang the doorbell. "I forget exactly how we're related. I think it's through your great-uncle Hjalmar Eugene. Or maybe it's *my* great-uncle Hjalmar Eugene. Either way, I'm sure he was great. Because he was a superhero."

I gave Dad a courtesy laugh. "How did Uncle John know to call Grandpa?"

"Probably like the rest who are calling him," Dad said. "They just keep trying different places until somebody picks up the phone."

Two months ago, we'd been attacked by a family of supervillains known as the Joneses. Benny and I, with help from our superfriend Juanita Johnson, had been able to stop them in Split Rock, but not before the villains had stolen everyone's superpowers.

I guess technically we still had superpowers, although I don't think I'd call them super. My brother could change his belly button from an innie to an outie. Dad could burp in Russian. I could strike matches on polyester, not just on matchboxes.

We weren't exactly what you'd call a threat.

And it didn't just happen to us. We'd started getting calls a few days after the attack. The Joneses had attacked superheroes everywhere. Most of our relatives had gone missing, but a few managed to escape. All of them had lost their powers, just like us. Since everybody in Split Rock was still accounted for, that became our home base. One by one, superheroes started gathering at Split Rock.

Gathering to hunker down.

Dad rang the doorbell again. Candlelight flickered inside the house. A voice called out, "Sorry, it's hard for me to get up. Let yourselves in."

Dad looked at me and raised his eyebrows. He opened the door, and we entered the house.

Things were as rundown inside as they were outside. Light from several candles bathed the room in shadows. Stacks of newspapers, magazines, and grocery sacks sat on top of every flat surface. A collection of stuffed animals rested on boxes in one corner. They seemed to stare at me with empty eyes. A dishwasher lay on its side against the far wall. A large vase containing a dead cactus perched on top.

An old man sat in the front room. Crutches lay on the floor next to him, and he had one leg propped up on a milk crate. A cast covered his leg from ankle to knee. Five toes stuck out of the white plaster like little mushrooms. He had a blanket draped across his lap and a bandage wrapped around his head that covered one eye and half his face. White whiskers poked out around his jaw and chin. He looked familiar. I must have seen him at one of our family's many reunions.

Dad walked across the room and held out his hand. "Hubert Bailey," he said. "I don't think we've met. I'm the great-grandson of Gjorts Ingavald Bailey."

The older man leaned forward and shook hands with Dad. "John Bailey," he said. "Son of Hjalmar Eugene. Sorry for not getting up. The doctor says I shouldn't put any weight on this leg for at least another week."

Uncle John sat back and motioned with his hand. "Please, have a seat. My nephew should be out in a moment."

I looked around. An old sofa sat against the wall by us, but a large stuffed moose rested on top of it. Not just a moose's head, but an entire stuffed moose. Someone had positioned a cone-shaped party hat between the moose's antlers.

"Yes, well uh . . . ," Dad said. "We're fine standing. How are things with you?" He motioned toward the cast. "Is that from the attack?"

Uncle John nodded. "I was on the roof hanging up our decorations for National Peanut Month. There was a flash of light, and suddenly I don't have my powers. I'm a Stretcher—or rather, I used to be. I'd gotten on the roof by stretching, so there I was, stuck up there without a ladder. I hit a patch of ice, and the next thing I knew I was waking up in the hospital with this." He motioned to his leg. "I got out of the hospital a day later and found my nephew, who had managed to avoid being captured. Of course we immediately assumed it was the Johnsons."

The Johnsons are another family of superheroes. For years, members of our two families had been fighting—in every major city in the country—with both families claiming to be the real superheroes. I'd thought Juanita Johnson was a villain, until she became my friend.

"But the Johnsons had gone missing just like us, and when we finally found you all up in Split Rock . . . well, you told us it wasn't the Johnsons. That's when we started looking for this third family. The Joneses."

I had been staring at all the crazy stuff in the room, but this comment focused my attention back to the conversation. "Have you found anything? About the Joneses, I mean?"

The Joneses. The real family of supervillains, they had kept the Johnsons and the Baileys fighting for decades. They'd stayed hidden in the shadows, doing who-knows-what while the superheroes fought among themselves.

Uncle John shook his head. "Haven't found a thing. It's like they don't even exist. We're still chasing down a few

MARION JENSEN'S
hilarious and heartfelt super (well, almost) hero stories

DIVIDED THEY'RE NOTHING. TOGETHER, THEY'RE . . .
ALMOST SUPER
MARION JENSEN

THEIR POWERS ARE GONE. NOW THEY'RE . . .
SEARCHING FOR SUPER
MARION JENSEN

www.harpercollinschildrens.com

HARPER
An Imprint of HarperCollinsPublishers

leads, and . . . well, my nephew and I, we're working on a few other ideas."

I was starting to like Uncle John. Only two Baileys had survived the attack here in Three Forks, but it sounded like instead of hunkering down, they were doing something. They were fighting back. In Split Rock, we had almost eighty Baileys and Johnsons gathered from all over the country, and all we'd managed to do was perfect the art of hiding.

"We've been able to piece together what happened," Dad said. "After they took away everybody's powers, the Joneses rounded everyone up and took them."

"Took them? Took them where?"

Dad shook his head. "We don't know. One Bailey from Nebraska said that no one was hurt, but he watched his family get loaded into a bus. The bus just drove away."

Uncle John rubbed the stubble on his jaw. "We've got to do something. All of these missing superheroes. Super-villains hiding and plotting, plotting and scheming." Uncle John looked me in the eye, his voice low and serious. "It's only a matter of time before everything falls apart."